Praise for *Braised Pork*

"Produces its own kind of mind trip . . . Written with a shimmering lightness." —*Wall Street Journal*

"A startlingly original debut . . . While it's easy to see that *Braised Pork* borrows something of Haruki Murakami's brand of strange melancholia, there's a startlingly original imagination of its own at work here . . . A sensitive portrait of alienated young womanhood." —*Guardian* (UK)

"The premise itself is intriguing enough, but the real magic is in watching Jia Jia stretch her limbs as she leaves behind a rather restrictive marriage and encounters places and people she never imagined. Come for the mystery, stay for self-discovery of a liberated woman." —*Literary Hub*

"Outstanding . . . Unforgettable . . . There is a kind of magic in the way the reader is also constantly submerged with Jia Jia for just long enough, before catching breath on the surface . . . Utterly original . . . A unique, metaphysical, and surreal tale of a woman that seeks answers in a world that has so often betrayed her with silence." —*Asian Review of Books*

T0025554

"Bold yet understated, *Braised Pork* is the debut of a supremely confident and gifted writer."

—Katie Kitamura, author of *A Separation*

"This exquisite novel is many things: a detective story in which the real object of pursuit is how one makes meaning of a sometimes ineffable existence; a meditation on the talismanic power of art and the indefatigability of the human spirit; and a many-faceted, perfectly cut gem of psychological portraiture set in well-wrought sentences burnished to a gorgeous luster. The emotions in this book keep pace with you, shadowing you with a quiet intensity, until in the last stretch they overtake you completely."

—Matthew Thomas, *New York Times*-bestselling author of *We Are Not Ourselves*

"Yu is a fantastic storyteller. The prose is sly and controlled, yet page after page, I found myself spellbound by a story that does what all writers hope to do, which is to make the familiar unfamiliar."

—Weike Wang, author of *Chemistry*

"What a singular, slippery, transfixing novel this is. An Yu achieves a hypnotizing emotional clarity as she takes her narrator ever further from a stifling life in Beijing into a watery realm unlike any I've read before."

—Idra Novey, author of *Those Who Knew*

"*Braised Pork* is mesmerizing, incisive, and utterly disarming. An Yu writes beautifully about loneliness, the experience of isolation—from others, from one's own past—and the possibility of human connection, however fragile."

—Rosie Price, author of *What Red Was*

"What a voice An Yu unfurls in *Braised Pork*. So elegant and poised, so tuned to the great mysteries of love and loss. Like a breeze on a still day, hers is a sound I didn't know I needed until I felt it. *Braised Pork* is a major debut."

—John Freeman, author of *Dictionary of the Undoing*

BRAISED PORK

AN YU

Braised Pork

Grove Press
New York

First published in in Great Britain in 2020 by Harvill Secker, an imprint of Penguin Random House UK

Published simultaneously in Canada
Printed in the United States of America

First Grove Atlantic hardcover edition: April 2020
First Grove Atlantic paperback edition: April 2021

Library of Congress Cataloging-in-Publication data is available for this title.

ISBN 978-0-8021-4872-8
eISBN 978-0-8021-4873-5

Grove Press
an imprint of Grove Atlantic
154 West 14th Street
New York, NY 10011

Distributed by Publishers Group West

groveatlantic.com

21 22 23 24   10 9 8 7 6 5 4 3 2 1

BRAISED PORK

1

The orange scarf slid from Jia Jia's shoulder and dropped into the bath. It sank and turned darker in colour, hovering by Chen Hang's head, like a goldfish. A few minutes earlier, Jia Jia had walked into the bathroom, a scarf draped on each shoulder, to ask for her husband's preference. Instead she had found him crouching, face down in the half-filled tub, his rump sticking out from the water.

'Oh! Lovely, are you trying to wash your hair?' was what she had asked him.

She knew well that he would not pull such a joke on her. But was it even possible for a grown man to drown in this tub? She checked his wrist for a pulse and bent to see whether there were bubbles coming out of his nose. She called his name, stepped into the bath and grabbed him by his torso to lift him, so that at least he could be the right way up. But he refused to budge, rigid like a broken robot.

The ambulance was on its way, or so they said. Jia Jia sank to her knees on the beige-tiled floor. She pulled the plug so the water could drain. It was the only thing she could think of doing now; maybe, without the water, Chen Hang would be able to breathe again. Crossing her arms on the rim of the bath, Jia Jia observed her husband's body as if he were a sculpture in a museum. She had never seen such stillness. She was certain that this was the first moment of silence she had spent with him in their four years of marriage: even when they slept, there were always sounds – his snoring, the air conditioning, cars on the streets. But she could not hear anything now. His crouching body appeared to be growing greyer and thinner, like dried and unglazed clay that was going to fall apart. Jia Jia felt suddenly like vomiting, realising that she had not been breathing either. She covered her mouth with her palm and tried to think about something else. She thought about how long it took for a body to grow cold after death. A few minutes? An hour? A few hours? She did not know. The humidity pressed down like hands on her throat, and the marble bathroom that had always been far too large seemed too small in this moment, suffocating for the two of them. It became clear to Jia Jia that Chen Hang must not have considered, not even for a moment, that such a place was improper for a death. He had not thought about his wife, who was going to be the first to find him, who was going to be alone when she did, and who would certainly be forced to wait before anyone else would join her in that bathroom. He had not pictured her in those few minutes after discovering him there, naked and dead, because if he had, he would surely have chosen another way.

During their breakfast that morning, Chen Hang had muttered, with a sigh and a mouthful of pickled cucumber, that perhaps it would be a good idea to resume their annual trip to Sanya. This was the first time anything encouraging had come out of his mouth for weeks. He had called off their holiday the previous year for unspecified reasons – presentiments, Jia Jia had feared, of his increasing lack of interest in her, and their marriage. He had never loved her, no, she knew that much. She was not a fool. But they had promised each other a lifelong partnership, held together if not by love, then by their declared intention to have a family. And so as long as he had assured her that he intended to remain married to her, everything else had been forgivable.

'When will we go?' Jia Jia had responded immediately, Chen Hang still chewing on the cucumber. 'I'll start packing after breakfast.'

'Whenever you like. I'm going to have a bath.'

'A bath?'

Jia Jia knew that Chen Hang had never been a man to have baths: he found no pleasure in soaking himself in hot water and preferred to shower, believing it led to cleaner results. She wanted to enquire further – she quickly swallowed her food, drank some water, and opened her mouth to speak – but decided to keep her silence for fear of irritating him with her questions and forcing him into a bad mood so early in the day.

'Don't pack too much,' he warned her, bringing the bowl of congee to his mouth and eating what was left in one gulp.

Jia Jia heard him put in the plug and start the water. It was November and she had just finished organising their wardrobes for winter. She opened his suitcase, mounted a chair, and reached into the upper compartment of the wardrobe for his summer clothes, refusing to let herself be distracted for fear of forgetting something of his. She was not going to let that ruin their trip. Let him have his bath, she decided, let him have his time alone.

By this point in their marriage, packing for Chen Hang could not have been simpler. The first time Jia Jia had prepared his suitcase for him, for their honeymoon, it had been a disaster. She had taken too many pairs of socks and forgotten his chess set. After that trip, she had quickly learned to arrange his suitcase to his liking: to roll the underwear and fold the polo shirts, arrange the chess set so that it would be nestled safely even after the suitcase was checked in, and leave a small space in the upper right-hand corner for his cigars, which he would pick out himself.

Packing her own belongings was more challenging this time. She had not been able to shop for new clothes – something Chen Hang always told her to do before they travelled.

'Go shopping,' he would say. 'Get some of that new stuff in the windows. You'll look nice for the beach. And you'll be happy.'

Maybe she should go shopping tomorrow. But Chen Hang had explicitly told her not to pack too much. Was there a financial issue? Was something going wrong with his business? Again she wanted to interrupt his bath and ask him. *Why are you having a bath? You never have baths. Is something wrong at work?* She was his wife, not his mistress, she had the right to know. But she felt afraid, as she often was with him, to dig up something that he would rather have kept buried.

Ultimately she decided to check on him anyway, to see if the bath had soothed him. Perhaps he might even open up to her naturally. So she picked out the two scarves, one orange and one floral, waited a few more minutes, rehearsed her smile, and gently pushed open the bathroom door.

She should have asked him at the very beginning, at the breakfast table. Now, her questions had to be swallowed back into her stomach. In fact, in that way, nothing had really changed, and this thought made Jia Jia feel insuppressible resentment and disgust towards the man she had let herself be married to. She ran to the toilet and vomited, unable to hold it in any more, her eyes tightly shut. He had betrayed her. Abandoned her. Failed to honour the one thing he had promised her. Everything about him became pitifully repellent; his brows contracted even in death, belly hanging like a pouch, head balding.

When she lifted her head, she noticed a piece of paper resting on a pile of towels near the sink. The paper was folded down the middle, opening and closing slightly in the stillness of the bathroom. It was as if the paper were alive. Jia Jia reached for it, revealing a drawing of a figure – a fish's body with a man's head. It was sketched by Chen Hang – she knew his crude style well enough.

The body of the creature had a curved spine through its centre and scales across the surface. Even from a rough sketch, it was evident that the large tail was powerful. The picture had been drawn in a rush, but the human part of it, unlike the rest, was handled with a great deal of precision. The head seemed to be a detailed portrait, everything was there: the wrinkles, the nose hair that stuck out a little, the swollen bags under its eyes. It was the head of a man whose eyes looked straight through the viewer towards a distant horizon. It resembled an ID photograph, neither laughing nor frowning. Nothing about the face was special except perhaps for the overly large and bare forehead. It showed no signs of a curious past or an exciting future.

Jia Jia remembered a dream that Chen Hang had told her about. He had been in Tibet, alone, for what he had called 'a spiritual escape from all this crap'. Though Chen Hang was not a religious man, beyond tossing money into donation boxes whenever he was in a temple or a church, he would go, periodically, on these trips by himself. Jia Jia knew that he needed them, but for what, she would rather not consider. She often reassured herself that she was his wife, the woman of his home, and he was a man who had selected his life partner with much consideration, a man who would never desert the woman he had chosen, even if at times his heart rested in someone else's bed. So for every one of his trips, Jia Jia had packed for him, sent him out the door, and waited for him to return.

This recent trip, perhaps a month ago, had been Chen Hang's first time in Tibet. One night while he was there, he had called Jia Jia and described a man who had appeared in his dream.

'He was barely a man,' he said. 'In fact, he was a small fish served on a plate, and everybody was eating it. We ate it all, every last piece of meat. Even the bones. But just when we started digging into the head,

it began to talk. Boy, was I scared! I'm surprised that
didn't wake me up. When it began to speak, I noticed
that it wasn't a fish. It was a man. The man was talking,
laughing, and telling us that he was late and we should
not wait for him to begin our meals. I can still hear
his roaring laugh.'

He had not remembered the rest of the dream and
he had not known who the man was. Jia Jia did not
give it too much thought at the time. The only thing
she did remember thinking was that Chen Hang must
have been alone for him to call her in the middle of
the night, that at least on this trip there had not been
another woman in his bed. In fact, she had forgotten
entirely about his dream until now, because after Chen
Hang returned from Tibet, he had not spoken about
the fish or the man again.

2

L eo stood alone behind the dark wooden counter of his bar, preparing a drink for his last customer. He wore a white shirt under a black vest with a burgundy bow tie, his sleeves rolled up to his elbows, hands damp from washing glasses. On the record player, Billie Holiday came to an end and he slowly wiped his hands and replaced her with Chet Baker. He always made sure to be calm and well-mannered, limiting his movements only to what was necessary for his work – a skill he had taken years to perfect. He rarely laughed loudly, but was never unfriendly, occasionally engaging in conversation when the bar was not busy. No one knew his real name; being 'Leo' was enough for him. He enjoyed that kind of secrecy – a professional, detached persona he could have in his bar. And as an added benefit, having an English name lent the place an air of sophistication.

The night had slowed and only one customer remained sitting at the counter. She was a woman in her early thirties who had visited the bar almost every evening in the past weeks. Leo knew her late husband, Chen Hang. The couple lived in the apartment compound across the road – the husband's office was nearby as well – so he had been a regular at the bar. Sometimes he came alone, but mostly with others. Very occasionally, he brought his wife with him, but she never stayed longer than the time she needed to finish a single glass of wine. She only drank wine.

Leo always made sure to observe his customers closely and took pleasure in being able to tell what mood they were in, whether they were accompanied by business clients or friends, and how they wanted him to speak to them. He remembered Chen Hang clearly: a clean-shaven man, dark-skinned even in winter, with only occasional hints of southern tones in his Mandarin. Most people would not have questioned his roots but Leo, born and raised in Beijing, had been in the people-watching business of bartending for years. Chen Hang was tall for a southerner, with broad shoulders and a strong physique. But every time he stepped out of the bar he lowered his head, lifted his shoulders, and sped up his footsteps ever so slightly. No matter how many villas and apartments he owned, he would never stroll the city streets like they were his own: a trait that was distinctly 'Beijingese', even for its poorest citizens. He had never acquired that particular sense of entitlement.

His wife was different. There was something about her that Leo could not decipher, a kind of aloofness that he found to be refreshing, as if all the world's interactions had nothing to do with her. Though she was not particularly striking and rather short, her clean features, small face and sloping shoulders reminded Leo of women in ancient ink paintings. Not beautiful, but incredibly feminine. Chen Hang seemed to have recognised that youth and beauty are transient, and so he had chosen her to be his wife; a gracious wife, the kind that a man would take to a dinner party and find, even when his wife was older, that he had become the centre of attention because he had the finest, most tasteful accessory. When he had brought her to the bar, it had been to show his success not only in business but in family as well. Her composure was permanent, and her smile always appeared elegant to Leo, despite her front teeth sticking out a little. It was as if a lid had been set over her emotions, and even if she was boiling inside, the lid held strong.

Since Chen Hang's death, she had started turning up at the bar fifteen minutes or so before closing time, forcing Leo to keep the place open for a while longer. She would push the door just enough for her thin body to slide through the gap and then proceed to the end of the counter, put her bag on the seat next to her, order a glass of wine, and loosen her bun to let her hair down. Most of the time, she was drunk already. At first, it was difficult for Leo to tell, as she never spoke to anyone and her movements were always rather graceful. It was not until she arrived sober one night that he saw a clear difference in her behaviour. She went through her whole routine – end of the counter, bag on the stool, one drink, hair down – but then she took out a pile of paper and put on a pair of reading glasses. It was not really the reading that gave away her sobriety but rather the focused serenity of her expression: at once curious and determined, like a child who was just beginning to read her first novel.

Tonight, though, she was more intoxicated than usual. She sat on the first seat she stumbled upon, tossing her bag on the floor. She asked for a glass of brandy and Leo served it to her along with a glass of water. With her eyes fixed on the drink, she bent over, lowered her lips to the rim and took a sip.

'Ah … yes, that's better. I prefer something strong. Don't you?' she said.

'I always have a glass of this brandy before going to bed,' Leo responded.

'No, not just before bed. I mean, I don't sleep much anyway.' She took another sip, studied her blurry reflection in the glass, and made a few dabs at her eye bags with her finger. 'I suppose I just got into the habit of drinking wine. You see, it's rather elegant, for a woman like me. But sometimes I just need something with more of a punch.' She lifted her bag from the floor and placed it on the stool. 'Now please save my seat, I need to get some air.'

'The air isn't so fresh tonight,' said Leo.

She fished out an anti-pollution mask from her pocket and waved it at Leo before pushing the door open.

It was snowing and rather cold, even for a December night in Beijing. The haze contaminated the snow as it descended in flakes the size of sunflower seeds. By one a.m., the road had settled to a slumber under a light grey canopy. Jia Jia hesitated and took a breath, allowing winter to fill her lungs before slowly letting it out. She thought about putting the mask on, changed her mind, and stuffed it back into her pocket. She lit a cigarette and listened to the sleeping city. It was oddly soundless tonight, which suited the dark, deep sky. Her apartment building stood right across the street, gigantic and forbidding.

It had been a month. The paramedics had not needed to transfer Chen Hang to the hospital to pronounce him deceased. But even after extensive investigation, the hospital could not determine the cause of death. Chen Hang's old parents came to Beijing from Fujian and, after a week, decided that it was unacceptable to delay their son's funeral any longer, and that Chen Hang was to join their family graveyard at once (otherwise his soul would be lost for ever). Besides, they themselves had spent too much time in a hotel in Beijing, and his mother could not sleep in a bed that was not her own. So Chen Hang's father had declared, with an authoritative slap on a table, that the cause of death on his son's death certificate was to be left unknown. He was dead, it did not matter how. He did not want them meddling with his son's body any more. The old couple wrapped the urn with a piece of grey cloth and carefully placed it in their bag. They refused to bring Jia Jia home with them for the funeral, calling her a curse, and demanding that she have nothing to do with the Chen family again.

It was all right. She had not wanted to go anyway.

Since then, everything else around her seemed to have moved on uncompromisingly. She learned from Chen Hang's lawyer that her husband, with all his wealth, had left her nothing but the apartment where they lived and her allowance of sixty thousand yuan, transferred to her bank account for the winter. He had written a will when they first got married, endowing most of his assets to his own family.

At his best, Chen Hang had provided for her; but in death he had made no provision. Jia Jia had swiftly come to understand that the past years of her life, the best years of her life, had been wasted and taken by a selfish man to his death, wrapped up into that urn and transported back to a graveyard where she, according to his family, had no right to enter. She should have given him a child sooner. That way, he would have cared more for her. But she had still been young when they married, and when she turned thirty and felt as though she was ready, a certain distance had begun to grow between them. It had not been clear to her back then, but now she saw that the foundation of their marriage had been disintegrating before his death. Those nights that he had spent elsewhere, the trip he had cancelled, the holidays he had taken without her. It was all right, she had told herself, *in time things will be fixed*. But where did all that leave her now? She felt homeless, ridiculous for having ever imagined that Chen Hang was going to give her a home. An empty apartment was not a home.

She had considered selling the apartment, but Chen Hang had been adamant that owning property was the safest investment, so she had contacted an agent to find her a tenant. The agent told her that the apartment was too large to be desirable for white-collar professionals who were mostly single or had small families. Larger families preferred to steer away from the Central Business District. *Fine*, she conceded, *list it for sale too*. Quite quickly, the agent had found a buyer who had offered her a fair price on the property, after which she had studied the contract in detail over a drink one night, but something had gone wrong

with the mortgage application and the buyer had
withdrawn.

Apart from an un-rentable, un-sellable apartment,
some cash, and a drawing of a fish-man, Jia Jia felt that
she did not own anything; that even these things were
not hers because they had all once belonged to her
husband. She frantically searched the rooms for something she could truly call her own. It had given her
comfort to find a few of her old paintings hanging on
the wall and stacked in the extra bathroom.

Chen Hang had been supportive of her painting –
until she had tried to sell her work at her friend's
gallery.

'Jia Jia, I remember talking to you about this,' he
had said to her. 'I don't want you to go out in the
world and struggle to make money. Let me provide for
my wife. Yes, you can paint! But I don't understand
why you feel you must go out and sell your paintings.
Like those struggling artists.'

She was sitting on the sofa in the living room, while
he paced around looking down at her.

'It looks bad,' he added.

With that, her career had become a hobby.

Jia Jia took one last puff on her cigarette and returned
to the bar. She thought the cold air had cleared her
head a little. The barman was wiping some glasses and
organising them back in place on the shelves. He had

large hands with long thin fingers, joints bulging out a little, like bamboo.

'Can I get you something else?' he asked.

'You're already cleaning up. I've had too much to drink.'

'Dishwashing is my way of meditating.' He tapped his index finger on his temple twice and winked. 'Mind if I join you?' he asked, lifting two glasses in one hand and an almost empty bottle of brandy in the other.

He poured and they touched glasses.

'I heard about your husband,' he said apologetically.

'Are you married?' Jia Jia said as she leaned across the counter to look at his name tag. 'Leo?'

'Certainly not,' Leo said.

'Why not?' she asked. He appeared to be thinking and did not answer her immediately. 'Oh, forget about it,' she said. 'I'm a fool to ask you, Mr Leo with an English name. There's no rush for you men. That's how you pronounce it, right? Lee-oh?' She slouched on her stool. 'But you must get married eventually. You must have a home to go back to after you close your bar. I'd hate to see you become a lonely old man, Mr Leo.'

'Did you feel at home when you were with him?' Leo asked, his eyes fixed on hers.

Jia Jia could not respond immediately; she was startled that he was provoking her like that, and not quite sure what he meant. Had Chen Hang told him, during one of his nights here, that he had lost interest in his wife? Or was it something that Leo had picked up from watching them while they were at his bar? Jia Jia's hand froze for a moment, but before Leo had a chance to notice, she brought her drink up to her lips. The lights hanging above the counter abruptly went off.

'I'm sorry.' Leo went to the corner of the room for the fuse box.

'Can I smoke in here?' Jia Jia asked as she fumbled for the new pack of cigarettes in her bag.

'When nobody else is here, you can,' he said.

Jia Jia rested a cigarette between her fingers. 'He gave me an apartment, you know?' she said after a few moments, bringing the cigarette to her lips and lighting it. 'Quite an impressive one, big and everything. It was nice of him to do that. Don't you think?'

A feeble light came on and Leo returned to the bar.

'This is the best I can do,' he said, pointing to the light. 'We'll have to wait a bit before trying to reset the breaker again.'

'Don't worry, I'm about to leave anyway.'

Jia Jia had wanted to order another drink. But what on earth was she doing, squandering money at expensive bars, as if Chen Hang would refill her bank account in a few months? And where had she left her pride, still hoping that Chen Hang would provide for her? Abruptly, she put her cigarette out, asked for the bill, stuffing an extra hundred-yuan note into Leo's hands as she paid. She swept up her belongings and left, concerned that the one hundred was not enough for the extra glass of brandy he had poured her. She would pay him back next time.

The pavements were empty and it had stopped snowing. Jia Jia slowed her footsteps, walking back across the street to her apartment, where she had a long shower and lay down. In bed, she began to weep beneath her blanket. The fan in the air purifier turned more furiously. Outside her window, buildings blurred as smog accumulated once again. And she kept crying, silently, occasionally choking while trying to catch her breath, as if, even in her desolation, she was too afraid to disturb the wintry silence.

3

When Jia Jia woke, it was still dark. She sat up and swept for her slippers with her feet. They were not there. She reached a bit further but found nothing. Looking down at the floor, she discovered that it did not exist any more, and what replaced it was the surface of a deep sea, as if she was sitting on the edge of a ship watching the reflection of the starless sky in the water. The darkness rippled like silk. She lifted herself from the bed and stepped onto what used to be the floor, falling into a sudden wet chill that was surely cold water. She immediately turned to grab for the bed, but it was no longer above her. Submerged in water, she searched for anything to hold on to. She held her breath and swam, deep, deeper.

Time became indistinct and irrelevant. Jia Jia did not know in what direction she was swimming. She could not see her body. If she was travelling down, once she reached the bottom of her building, would she find the ground again? It was worth a try, she thought. After what felt like a long time, a white ray of light penetrated the water. The sun! It must be the sun rising in the distance. Refracted, the light seemed alien, as though it belonged in a different dimension, but Jia Jia swam towards it anyway, pulling at and ripping off her pyjamas, crying for help, her voice muffled.

As she was nearing the light, she spotted a small silver creature beneath her, swimming around in circles. She thought she could make out a tiny fish with a sharp tail, shining like glitter. It swam wildly – a fry just learning how to flap its fins.

Jia Jia shifted her focus back to the light and pushed towards it, leaving the silver fish behind. The light grew brighter. She rose out of the water, finding herself sitting on the floor of her apartment, naked, pyjamas in a heap, frozen to the core. The morning sun pierced the blind, the sky was a pale blue now, and a group of middle-aged women were already gathered outside in the park dancing to disco tunes.

Jia Jia's eyes gradually adjusted to the light. She was shaking. With an automatic gesture she reached for the drawing on the bedside table. Relieved to find it still dry, she leaned her head against the bed and studied the fish-man. She saw lifelessness in its eyes, like prey that was being hunted and had already given up.

Jia Jia folded the drawing, though she was unable to erase the image from her mind. The water, what was it? She could not remember what it looked like any more, only the stinging cold that it had left on her skin. The heater must have broken during the night. A bitter chill remained. The apartment was too big. She had to move out, she decided, as soon as she could. She could not bear being alone in this place.

Jia Jia could not remember the last time she had admitted, even to herself, that she was truly afraid of something. It was not because she never experienced fear, because of course she did, but she had learned very young that her vulnerabilities would only lead to more trouble for her family: more worry for her grandmother, more tears for her aunt, more concerned late-night whispers between the two of them.

The day that her mother died, Jia Jia had just started middle school.

That evening, peeping through the door to the bedroom where her grandmother wept into her pillow in silence, her legs hanging from the edge of the bed, Jia Jia had learned to do the same.

Now she tried to get up but found herself unable to summon the energy to rise. She wrapped the duvet around her body and sat for hours on the wooden floor, wishing that the day would stop for a moment and wait for her. She closed her eyes and searched for memories of her mother. She had not done this for a long time. The memories were fragmented and faint, just as they always were. Jia Jia was sure that these memories had felt like reality once, that at a distinct moment in the past there had been an intensity and lucidity to them. But when? She could not say any more. She could not remember the details, only the existence of details.

In the afternoon, Jia Jia decided to go to her grandmother's. She wanted a distraction, something to occupy her mind and lift her up from the floor. She got dressed and boarded the 139 bus towards Jianguomen. It would take longer than the subway, but she felt better able to breathe above ground. Jia Jia managed to find a seat towards the back, next to a mother and a girl. The mother held the girl's schoolbag on her lap and had a few plastic bags of groceries near her feet. The two did not speak much during the journey, only once when the mother unscrewed the top off an insulated bottle, poured some warm water into it, and held it up to her daughter's lips.

'You need to drink more water,' she said.

The girl, keeping her eyes fixed on a picture book in her lap, opened her mouth for her mother to feed her. When Jia Jia got off the bus, the mother and daughter rode on.

Jia Jia had grown up in a compact three-bedroom apartment with her grandmother and her aunt. It was in an old brick building, on the second floor, overlooking a courtyard. Her grandparents' apartment had

been consigned to them by their employer, and when
her grandfather passed away, her aunt had moved in
to take care of her grandmother. Then, when her aunt
married Li Chang, he joined them too. Through the
years, the courtyard had become crowded with parked
cars and there were fewer bikes lying around than
there had been in Jia Jia's childhood. A group of
women walked out of the front gate just as Jia Jia
entered. She did not recognise them. When she was
young, she thought that the families who lived in this
building would never leave; they had seemed so rooted
to this piece of land, as if they had sprouted from it,
like trees.

Jia Jia pushed open the metal door, stamped hard
on the floor to switch on the lights, and climbed up
the stairs. There were more advertisements on the
stairway walls, posters layering over the old ones.
Someone had written 'car rental' followed by a phone
number directly onto the wall.

She knocked on the door and her aunt greeted her.

'Look at my new aquarium!' her aunt said. She
slanted her body so that Jia Jia could squeeze past the
shoe cabinet and into the room.

There was a large aquarium in the living room,
standing more than a head taller than Jia Jia. Different
species of fish swam inside, eyes big and round, lost
and disconcerted. But even with so many fish, the
tank looked oddly vacant.

'Did you get any coral?' Jia Jia asked, putting down her bag on the sofa.

'It's coming tomorrow,' her aunt said, proudly looking at the tank as if it was her child.

Jia Jia's grandmother was shaking her head as she walked, with tiny steps, out of her room.

'We're just a normal family living in a normal apartment,' her grandmother said, her voice raspy with mucus, and her face scrunched into a displeased expression. 'Jia Jia, your aunt has a new idea every day, always trying to go with the trend. Look at how much space this thing is taking up!'

'Li Chang's at a meeting right now,' her aunt said to Jia Jia, ignoring the old woman. 'He and I have been working on a film project. Once I get my share of the money, I'll try to get you a nice little apartment, and an aquarium just like this. It should be a big sum this time.'

Jia Jia's aunt sat down and began rinsing and sterilising teacups with boiling water.

'The apartment you're in now is too big for you. You should sell it and invest in our project,' she continued. She picked three cups out with a pair of wooden tongs. 'Last night your uncle and I stayed at the Four Seasons to celebrate this film deal. More than one thousand yuan a night! Li Chang and I thought the lobby was so beautiful. Too bad it's winter, otherwise we would've had a drink on the terrace.'

'I thought you were opening a restaurant?' asked Jia Jia.

'We figured it's better to do something Li Chang's good at,' her aunt explained. 'The restaurant idea was a little foolish.'

Jia Jia's aunt had never been able to earn the life she wanted with her various business ventures. Chen Hang used to criticise her approach: he would flip his hand in the air, shake his head and declare that Jia Jia's aunt had set her sights too high, that she was too eager, that she idealised money too much. *You won't earn money by obsessing over it*, he would say, while he cracked a nut. But had he not been the same?

'How about you, my dear, what are your plans?' Jia Jia's aunt looked up from her tea set at her niece.

'I'm looking for somebody to rent or buy my apartment. Auntie, I think I should start painting again,' Jia Jia said. 'Sell my paintings.'

'Oh, get yourself a stable job,' her grandmother said, walking slowly behind the table to sit beside her daughter and making a shuffling sound with her slippers. She had been wearing those yellow polka-dotted slippers for more than ten years at least, and when the problems began with her knee joints, she had sewn fabric to the soles so that she could move more easily by sliding her feet along the floor. 'You should've listened to me,' her grandmother added with a sigh.

Jia Jia remembered, of course she did: she remembered her grandmother telling her to study something that would give her more job security. An 'iron rice bowl', her grandmother had called it. She breathed in deeply, knowing that there should not be any more debates over this matter, and that the old woman had already been through too much in her life. Anything coming out of Jia Jia's mouth, should she allow herself to open it now, was going to be too spiteful. So she said nothing. She had to control her temper. She could not allow her aunt and grandmother to detect the faltering feeling inside her.

'Let me ask if Li Chang has anything for you,' her aunt suggested.

'Make sure that it's proper work and that they won't cheat her,' Jia Jia's grandmother said.

'Ma,' her aunt began again. 'I know you don't like Li Chang, but he knows a lot of wealthy people who might like to order some art from Jia Jia.'

'I won't intervene any more,' her grandmother said with a forlorn expression. 'I don't know how the world today works. But having a practical skill is the safest bet. Look at you and Li Chang, still living in my apartment. He should have his own place by now.'

Then she rose from her seat to start cooking dinner, shaking her head as she slid away.

'Stay for dinner, Jia Jia,' her aunt said.

*

Just after nine p.m., Jia Jia roamed into Leo's bar. She did not speak at first: there was too much on her mind for it all to be organised into words. It had hit her, upon walking out of her grandmother's door, that she no longer had to abide by rules made by anybody else. She was not a child any more, and her grandmother's opinions, no matter how strong, were confined behind that door. She could walk anywhere now, answering to nobody. She had the opportunity to pursue her art, without Chen Hang there to tell her how bad it looked to others. It made her want to get a nice glass of champagne.

She called Leo over.

'A glass of the best champagne you have, please,' she told him.

'This one?' He opened the menu and pointed it out to her. 'It comes by the bottle usually. But I can give you a glass. Looks like you're in a celebratory mood today.'

'Oh, let's have the whole bottle then!' She laughed and tapped her finger on the name of the champagne.

If she were to support herself with her art, she wanted to feel free to walk around her home in an oversized T-shirt, face unwashed, hair trimmed short. Though even there, she imagined someone who would provide her with comfort regardless and bring her food from whichever restaurant she desired in that moment, even if it was on the other side of town. Yes!

She would make new memories with someone else, memories that would give her a home and fuel her work.

Leo returned with the bottle and opened it discreetly, releasing a soft hiss. He poured a glass out for her – cool, golden.

'Do you like art?' Jia Jia asked.

'I've always been more into music.'

'Will you write a song for me then?' She laughed.

Usually she was courteous with her laughter, but she wanted to be flirtatious, playful. She could not remember the last time she had expressed herself like this, not with a reaction to something but with an initiation. Leo smiled back to match her. His laugh was almost a chuckle.

'Have you ever written songs for your girlfriends?' she asked.

'Once, for my most recent ex. But she didn't like it.'

'Tell me about her.'

'Well …' He searched for a succinct way to answer a broad question. 'She was like a bad hangover.'

'So she gave you a headache.'

'Many. Bad ones.'

'Did you understand her? I mean, did you really *understand* who she was and why she did what she did?'

'Just because you understand someone doesn't make them any easier to deal with.' He placed the bottle in the ice bucket and draped a napkin over it.

Jia Jia considered that for a moment. 'I never understood my husband,' she said.

'Was he a complicated man?'

'Oh, not at all. He grew up in a poor but normal
family, worked hard, did well in business, married me,
and then died. Sounds like a simple life, right? But I
didn't even understand his simplicity.'

'Is that what you want? Simplicity?'

'I'm not sure any more.' She took a sip of the champagne. The bubbles were intense at first, like a loud
chord at the beginning of a symphony, but almost
immediately afterwards, harmony came to the tip of
her tongue.

He gave her a questioning look, requesting an
elaboration.

'It's like I've been walking up the walls of a tower
my whole life,' she explained, putting the glass down.
'My body parallel to the ground, and then, the world
turns and I'm standing straight up, and the tower is
lying flat on the ground. Everything is now distorted
but my head is up again, I'm walking forward. But the
truth is, I don't even know which way is up. Do you
understand what I'm getting at? The champagne is
good, very good, I must tell you.'

Before Leo could answer, some other customers
walked in, and Jia Jia gestured to him that it was all
right to pause their conversation. It was a party of
four: two men and two women. Both men wore suits

beneath their overcoats, one grey, the other navy; they had taken their ties off after work. The smaller of the women removed her fur coat and revealed a colourful halter top with a low neckline. She was loud. Before she even sat down in her seat, she had announced that she was a lawyer.

'Those boys didn't have a chance against me,' she bragged. 'I don't care if you're fighting in front of the club, but if you're going to punch *my* friend in front of *me*, then you're being foolish. I made sure that the kid got the sentence he deserved.'

'He was pretty young though, right?' the other woman asked.

'The kid was eighteen. Drove a Maserati.' She took out a thin cigar. 'His parents came to apologise and asked to settle. "We're so sorry, our boy needs to be taught a lesson," was what they said to me. So I responded, "Perfect, he's getting the correctional education he needs."'

She laughed loudly.

'You should've seen their faces!' she added.

And then they all laughed and ordered their drinks. Leo returned and quietly asked Jia Jia whether the loud group was bothering her.

'Quite the contrary,' she whispered back. 'Let them talk, they're funny.'

*

Jia Jia was still sitting in her seat when the bar closed. The four had left and the woman had never managed to light her cigar. Leo had remained occupied for the rest of the night, concentrating on making his cocktails. Jia Jia would occasionally observe his fingers while he was working: he was quite average-looking, but she found a certain appeal in the way he moved his hands. He must be a committed man, she thought, so dedicated to what he loved to do. His movements looked effortless – the kind of ease that was only attained after years of practice.

He cleaned up the last table and returned to the counter. Then he moved Jia Jia's bag and sat on the stool next to her – a surprising act of intimacy from a man who sustained a polite distance from others. Jia Jia turned her stool to face him.

'I've finished with the bottle. It's about time for me to go,' she said.

'Stay for another drink with me.' He reached over the counter for brandy and two glasses.

They drank in silence.

'Do you think I'm beautiful?' Jia Jia asked.

'You're like water. Your beauty is soft and quiet.'

'Will you stay with me tonight then? It'll be a good memory, I think, for us both.'

The pavement was wet with melted snow and parts of it were freezing over again as the temperature dropped. Leo closed the bar and the two of them walked in the direction of Jia Jia's apartment. The cleaner air from the day was gone now, and the city hid behind its mask.

4

Jia Jia sped up her footsteps as she passed the concierge, leaving Leo trailing behind. The doorman greeted her but she kept her chin slightly tucked into her scarf and did not stop until she was at the lift.

They were silent on the long ride up. Away from his bar, Leo's confidence had faded and his demeanour was uneasy. He seemed to be shorter and smaller. Inside the apartment, he slowly removed his coat and held on to it as Jia Jia threw hers on the sofa.

Sensing his mood, she took his coat with one hand and touched his arm with the other, encouraging him. He responded by pulling her into him as if he could now stop pretending to be timid. She felt her breasts against his chest; his lips reached out to meet hers. His breath tasted like fresh mint and she felt self-conscious that her own probably reeked of alcohol. She did not remember seeing him eat a mint.

The touch of his hands on her skin seeped into her pores like water. It was as if there was a place inside her that no one had reached before, and it had been shaken awake by this man's warm embrace. She had never felt such yearning for another person's body – it was beyond the flesh and the consciousness, it was not merely lust, neither was it love. Perhaps the best way to describe it, she thought, was like being a lone traveller in a desert, exhausted and desolate, when the most beautiful and fruitful peach tree blossomed in front of her.

But just as Leo lay her down in bed, a wave of guilt broke over Jia Jia. Someone else was invading Chen Hang's space and she was the only protector of it now. She wanted to ignore the thought, to chase it away, but with her back against the cold silk of the sheets that she had shared with her husband, she felt as though she was cheating on Chen Hang. Leo did not have the same moment of hesitation; he took off his bow tie, his vest, and finally his shirt, but he kept his trousers on, waiting for her to take them off for him. She ran her hands around his hips to his erect penis, all the time avoiding his eyes.

Everything about Leo made her husband's presence more tangible. Leo's skin was firmer, his bones were sharper, his hands were bigger. The outline of his body in the dark was strange and alien to her. He removed her trousers before unbuttoning her shirt – the opposite of what Chen Hang would have done. The feeling of him inside her was different. The feeling of her taking him in was different. The way he moved on top of her and the way his muscles tensed were, somehow, all so different.

Still, she pulled him hard towards her – this stranger who touched a part of her that had been entirely isolated from the world.

When Jia Jia woke up, Leo was gone from the room. Her first thought was that he had left, but then she heard him in the kitchen. She had wanted some time alone. She quickly washed her face and got dressed, and when she walked into the living room, she saw that Leo had already bought food and was boiling eggs.

'I have eggs in the fridge, you know,' Jia Jia said.

'I bought other food too.'

She looked at the clock, it was already past eleven.

'What time do you have to be at the bar to prepare?' she asked.

'Not until four or five. Nice painting over there.' He pointed towards the wall behind the sofa.

'Oh,' she hesitated. 'Thank you.'

She was unsure why she chose not to tell him that she was the artist. It was not a piece that she was particularly proud of, anyway. No one had complimented it before – she had only hung it two days ago to replace one that Chen Hang had bought from an art gallery off Rue du Bac in Paris.

Her painting was of a brown horse on a beach, looking back at something beyond the frame. The beach was muddy and rocky, and the waves were strong. She was never very skilled at making waves look realistic, although it was her favourite scenery to paint. As a student, she had saved up all of her money from her part-time job and gone on a trip to London, where she had spent hours in the National Gallery studying and trying to copy paintings that had waves in them. Still, she could not do it. Not in the way she wanted to, at least. There was something about the movement of the ocean and the semi-translucency of the water that she could not grasp; some balance between mystery and simplicity. After she graduated, she had even gone so far as to spend a week in a Taoist temple to learn about the behaviours of water.

So she was surprised that someone acknowledged her painting as a good one.

'Who chose the picture?' Leo asked.

'I did,' she said.

'I actually don't really like the ocean,' he said. He passed over a takeaway bowl of warm soya milk, a bag of fried dough sticks, and a plate of stir-fried lotus roots. 'There isn't really a particular reason, just never liked it as a kid.'

'My husband didn't like water either. He said that it was a dangerous and wild substance. It's very challenging to paint.' Jia Jia took a bite of a dough stick and studied her bite mark as she chewed.

'I can imagine.' Leo hesitated briefly. 'It must take a lot of practice. An old acquaintance of mine grew up near the coast, his dad is a fisherman. He studied art and paints incredible oceans, so that makes a lot of sense. He's been in and around water all his life. The guy sucks at everything else he paints though.'

'His dad is a fisherman? He allowed his son to study art?'

'Oh, no, of course not.' Leo laughed and shook his head at the recollection. 'His dad told him never to set foot in his house again.'

Jia Jia's own father had never opposed her studying art, but neither had he supported it. Worse – he was indifferent. Her father had left her mother when Jia Jia was five years old, and after that, when she lived with her mother and then with her grandmother, he would only invite her out for lunch once or twice a year. When she told him that she had been admitted to the Central Academy of Fine Arts, he merely acknowledged it and smiled, and continued to order food from the waitress. He might also have made a congratulatory remark, but it did not matter, because a year or two later, he had forgotten all about it again.

'I went to art school as well,' she told Leo.

He walked behind her and touched her shoulders with his hands.

'I overheard you talking about it in the bar once,' he said.

Leo's affection suddenly made her uneasy. The intensity from the night before had faded now, and the contact felt out of place. She quickly finished her breakfast and started going through the post. The monthly maintenance and heating bills had come – the first ones she had received since her husband's death. The electricity bill was also in the pile. The building's management must have felt sorry for sending the bills while she was mourning, so they had given them to her two weeks later than the usual date. The payment deadline, though, was still the same.

She opened up the envelopes and was almost offended to see that the total charges amounted to four thousand yuan. Heating constituted the bulk of it. Chen Hang would complain about spending too much on heating in the winter, but Jia Jia had always insisted on keeping the room temperature warm because she did not like to wear sweaters indoors. He was indignant at being a victim of the smog, too, not so much because of its health implications but because purifiers consumed a lot of electricity and that increased their monthly spending. It was she who had insisted on keeping the purifiers turned up high, and he had not denied her such indulgences.

Now that he was gone, paying four thousand yuan per month for the rest of the winter meant that Jia Jia really had to start making her own money. Had Chen Hang planned for her to be in this situation? Did he even consider it? Was it madness, her brief sliver of hope that she could support herself with her paint-ings? She had been out of work for years, lost her contacts, settled into life as the wife of Chen Hang. Perhaps there was nothing that she could do out there.

Leo must have noticed the concerned look on her face.

'Are you all right?' he asked.

'Yes,' she said without looking up at him, unwilling to continue the conversation further. She took out a pen and started doing calculations on a separate sheet of paper.

'Do you live around this area?' she asked Leo as she added the months up, pen scribbling.

'Not in the CBD. It's too pricey. I live a bit further away, near the embassy area. Still expensive, but—'

'You're right. I don't need four bedrooms for myself,' she said. 'It's awfully difficult to clean,' she quickly added, justifying herself.

Leo began telling her about the neighbourhood he lived in, but Jia Jia was absent-minded and responded with either short acknowledgements or nothing at all. She turned off the heat and the air purifier and threw on a sweater. She smoked cigarette after cigarette, all the time looking for cheap apartment rentals on the Internet. Eventually, Leo said goodbye and headed to the bar.

After the door closed behind him, Jia Jia pulled her laptop screen down and felt both relieved and abandoned once again. She thought about what was going on beneath her apartment; what other people were doing with their days. Office workers would be taking their lunch breaks by this time. In the past, Jia Jia would visit Chen Hang near his office and have lunch together with his employees. She had never really enjoyed it – the meals were rushed and the conversations filled with flattery – but now, she almost wanted that again. She missed that sense of routine.

She picked up the plates Leo had left on the table and began washing them. The ghost faces of the lotus roots glared up at her. Leo had not eaten all the fried dough, unlike her husband who would have finished everything on the table, even if he had not been hungry. No matter how much money Chen Hang made, he never ordered too much food unless it was for business, and when he did over-order, he would make sure to force everything down. With all his wealth, he never felt rich.

Jia Jia noticed that she smelt like cigarettes and turned on the shower. As she took off her clothes, she saw the plum-sized, greyish, kite-shaped birthmark on her left inner thigh. She had not thought of it with Leo, which was odd, because she never forgot about it. Though Chen Hang had never spoken about this mark, Jia Jia vividly recalled his expression when he first saw it. As if it were a pothole in the middle of a highway, he had steered his glance around and away from it. From then on, she had tried to cover up the stain with her hand or a piece of clothing every time it was exposed, especially when they were in bed, until after they got married and it became something that was unbearable for her to sustain, so she found sex positions that she thought would better shield the imperfection from her husband. She had pleaded with him to try them with her, pretending it was for her own pleasure.

She dug her fingernails into the birthmark as she closed her eyes and retraced Chen Hang's body with her mind, from his balding head, to his flat nose, to the hair below his navel, and to all that she had tried so desperately to please. To her surprise, she could barely remember his naked body any more, only the ugliness of it in that bath. Her thoughts returned to Leo, relieved that he had not turned on the lights the night before. She could almost convince herself that the distorted, dark patch of skin on her leg would not matter to him, that maybe, if he was the one holding her, it might even fade and disappear. She could not say why, he just seemed like the kind of man who healed, rather than wounded.

5

Jia Jia visited Leo's bar less often through December; she had to save her money. The few times she did go, she spent the night with Leo. Occasionally, he would stay for the day too, but mostly, he left after breakfast. Jia Jia's intense craving for his body continued to consume her each time, as if this empty cup of hers would never fill up.

She had not been able to move out of the apartment since the night she had fallen into the dark sea. On days when she did not see Leo – most days – she drank at home and stayed awake until dawn, waiting for it to appear again. She could not forget the deep waters and the little silver fish – did it have some connection to the fish-man? She thought that she would have to be alone to see the water again, but even when Leo was not there, the apartment did not transform and all she could feel under her feet were the stubborn wooden floors that she had picked out from an Italian vendor. She tried everything: wearing the same two-piece pyjama set that she had had on; putting the fish-man sketch on the floor. But nothing happened. Apart from staying in and waiting, she could not think of anything else to do.

She did start painting again. She dug out some of her old brushes and unused canvases from the storage room on Christmas morning while Leo was making breakfast.

'Merry Christmas,' he said, taking a canvas from her hand and replacing it with a glittery, silver bag.

'Oh, thank you. I didn't know you celebrated Christmas.' She had not bought him a present. In fact, she had not even been aware of the date. She had planned to spend the morning going to the 798 Art District, to the gallery where she had worked for a few years after university – and where in fact she had first encountered Chen Hang – to see if she could find a job of some sort that could pay the bills.

'I don't,' responded Leo. 'I don't like foreign holidays. But it's a good occasion to give you this.'

She opened the bag and saw a photography book titled *The Sea*. True to its name, the book was a collection of shots of tall ships riding against stormy waves, solitary lighthouses, and boundless seascapes that almost looked like oil paintings.

'This is beautiful,' said Jia Jia, closing the book and storing it on the shelf, next to Chen Hang's collection of photography books. She walked over to Leo and held his hand. 'What do you think, shall we go to 798?' she asked. 'For an exhibition? Perhaps a coffee?'

The exhibitions in Beijing were rarely much good, but she felt compelled to celebrate Christmas with Leo now that she had accepted a present from him. After breakfast, she tried to decide on what to wear. She must not dress too casually, but overdressing would attract too much attention. She put on a dark blue polo-neck and some black tailored trousers.

On their way to 798, she began dreading seeing her old colleagues, especially since she was going with Leo. She had not been back to the gallery since her husband's death, and she did not want to spend the afternoon hearing condolences.

Jia Jia had met Chen Hang during her first week there as a receptionist. He had called in one day to visit the owner and had given Jia Jia his business card before leaving. At the time, she had not had many friends there: the manager was older and married to her university roommate's brother, and the other younger employees had boyfriends their own age, many of whom had careers in art as well. Once she started dating Chen Hang, her colleagues distanced themselves from her, as if she belonged to a different category of woman: the practical kind who did not care for romance. She had never really minded this impression – she did not see it as shameful – but going back on a date with a man her own age would confirm to her colleagues that their idea of romance had been the correct one. They would think that it had taken her husband's death for Jia Jia to understand something they had known all along. That, to her, was more humiliating. So she guided Leo elsewhere.

They headed towards UCCA, a bigger gallery that seemed to be popular that day. The entrance was packed with young couples and parents who wanted to educate their children. There was a large banner outside with a portrait of a middle-aged man, an artist who worked with ink on paper. From the photo, no one would have ever guessed that the man was a painter: with his white shirt, brown blazer and cropped hair, his appearance resembled that of a businessman or a politician.

The gallery was as lively and crowded as it could get. People lined up side by side, moving along the walls from painting to painting like students waiting for food in a canteen. Every picture was largely the same but with slight differences in composition. Each one had a woman and some animals in it. Sometimes the women would be looking right, and other times they would be facing left with the same expression of indifference. The cows, the sheep, the birds and the rabbits in the paintings, however, always stared straight at the viewer.

After the exhibition, Jia Jia and Leo spent the rest of that afternoon setting up his bar. They did not talk much, and when he made any remarks about the exhibition, about how wonderful it was, she disagreed with most of them. When the bar opened, she said that she was tired and walked home alone. They had forgotten about the coffee.

Back home, Jia Jia placed the fish-man sketch next to a blank canvas and studied it. She wanted to paint it. Her idea was that the experience of reinterpreting Chen Hang's sketch as her own art would give her a clue or two about the fish-man and her husband's dream in Tibet. She had often done this when she found it difficult to relate to a piece of artwork – she would reproduce it onto her own canvas, and through this, understand what that piece meant to her.

The sketch looked easy enough to copy. After all, it was only the face that was intricate; the body could have been drawn by a child. She sketched the outline of the fish-man onto the canvas with a pencil. The light was shining from the upper-left corner, so she briefly shadowed out parts on the right side. She stepped back and observed the proportions – about a third for the head and the rest for the body. She would have to decide on the colours of the fish and Chen Hang's drawing gave no help there. The silver fish from the deep sea came to her mind. It was a good start, she thought. Next, she had to mix the paint for the background. She began with a vibrant blue, like the shallow parts of the ocean on a sunny day. It was challenging as always – the colours came out artificial, like food colouring. She put her brush down and imagined the sea in a transparent blue, constantly changing in hue when the waves moved in soft, quiet beats. She added some yellow to her paint and spread it neatly around the fish-man. Dipping a smaller brush into silver paint, and then mixing it with some grey, and finally with a dab of dark, muted green, she painted its body. She wanted it to be like Chen Hang's drawing, rough and unfinished, so she left it at the blocking stage and avoided adding too much detail.

Jia Jia was unable to paint the face. That part of the canvas, as if rejecting her, erased all the outlines and colours from her mind. Whenever she looked at the empty face of the fish-man, it was as if she had forgotten how to paint. She did not know where to put the eyes, what colour the lips should be, how much space the nose was supposed to occupy. Sure, she could measure out the proportions from Chen Hang's sketch and transfer it to her own canvas, but she had never liked to work that way. Even though she was copying, it still had to be *her* painting.

In the days following, she painted more. She took out six canvases and painted different versions of the fish-man. Sometimes she began with the body; other times with the face. But whenever she directed her brush to the empty oval where the face was supposed to be, her mind went blank, and she could not recall what kind of an expression the fish-man wore.

Only at night, when she lay in bed, would its face finally come to her, lucid and precise. She would jump up, go to her canvas, pick up her brush, and all the images would evaporate from her mind again. Once, she looked through the photography book that Leo had given her, but quickly remembered that it was entirely filled with landscape photos. Had someone given this collection to her when she was younger, it would have helped her tremendously. But now, it was not what she needed. She needed a face.

It was not until a cold and brisk January night, two weeks after the exhibition, when Jia Jia needed to step away from her paintings, that she made her way to Leo's bar again.

'I tried to call you,' said Leo as he watched Jia Jia sit down in her usual seat. 'How are you?'

'Oh, I'm doing well. I was away for a few days,' she lied.

Why did people ask each other how they were? Jia Jia wondered. *How are you* was a question that most of the time resulted in an untruthful response. She could not tell Leo that she was not well, not really. It was a dreadfully lonely experience to be asked, as if

she were being given a small rock to step on to cross
a deep, rough river.

She knew that by now Leo was able to tell whether
she wanted to talk or not. There had been times when
she had intentionally carried herself as though she
preferred to be treated as a normal customer. She
would greet him with a smile, sit down, order a drink,
end their exchange with a simple 'thank you' and proceed to read a book. She was never impolite in these
moments, but if it was just the two of them in the bar,
her behaviour exhibited a slight hint of uncertainty.
Tonight was not one of those nights. She did not want
to sit alone tonight.

'What do you want to drink?' asked Leo.

'How about something new and strong,' she said.
'That book you gave me is wonderful, I've been studying a lot from it. I dug out some of my old materials
and I've been trying to paint a fish.'

'A fish?'

'Well, not exactly. A fish-man.' She dragged the
word 'man' out a little.

He raised his eyes from zesting limes and looked at
her.

'My husband left a drawing for me,' Jia Jia explained.
'A fish-man drawing. It has a man's head with a body
that resembles a fish. You know, with scales and fins.
Ever since I put my hands on the drawing, I've been
having this feeling that I need to find out more about

it. It has quite an odd-looking face. I can show you next time. Anyway, I'm painting it now. I didn't think it would be so difficult to recreate.' She slouched over and rested her elbows on the counter.

'What do you mean, an odd-looking face?' Leo asked.

'I mean, I've been studying the drawing, but whenever I turn to my canvas and try to paint its face, my mind goes blank and I can't remember what it looks like. It's as if the fish-man doesn't want me to paint it. Weird, isn't it? Does this happen to you when you make cocktails?'

'I'm not quite sure. I do run out of ideas,' Leo said hesitantly. 'But painting is not the same as mixing drinks.'

Jia Jia shook her head. 'You're right. That's not it,' she said. 'I know exactly what I want it to look like, but I just can't paint it. It seems like the face only exists in my head, and it's always changing.'

'Why is it that he drew a fish-man, do you think?'

Jia Jia had been expecting this question from Leo. She started answering him almost before he had finished asking.

'Chen Hang said that the fish-man was in his dream once. The dream itself was a strange one. He couldn't remember most of it, but how could he draw the fish-man without remembering most of the dream?'

'So you know what you want to paint, but can't do it. He didn't remember the dream, but could sketch the fish-man in detail.'

Jia Jia nodded slowly.

'I would love to see the sketch some day,' Leo said. 'And, of course, your painting, when you succeed.'

Leo stayed with Jia Jia that night. She kept the door to the study closed and did not show him her paintings. She was not ready yet. She kept Chen Hang's sketch from Leo too; it felt like something that was too intimate, as if it was the one thing that was honest about Chen Hang. She could not explain why, but she knew that Chen Hang would have wanted to keep it hidden from others.

Early the next morning, Jia Jia's aunt paid her an unannounced visit. Jia Jia was brushing her teeth, so Leo answered the door. Her aunt was slender and tall, and she carried herself in such a youthful manner that Leo later told Jia Jia that he had mistaken her for one of Jia Jia's friends.

'Oh! It's very nice to meet you. I'm the girl's aunt. I watched her grow up,' Jia Jia heard her aunt say and saw, through the crack of the bathroom door, the woman poking her head inside the bedroom. 'I shouldn't have come so early. I wanted to talk to Jia Jia. Ah! Jia Jia's changed the painting. Beautiful, isn't it?'

'She has fine taste in art,' Leo responded.

'She painted this one about two, or maybe three years ago,' her aunt said. 'She's never happy with her own work.'

'Auntie, why didn't you call me?' Jia Jia hurried out from the bedroom, abashed at being caught in her husband's apartment with another man. She avoided looking at Leo. 'Did you stay at the Four Seasons again?'

'No, not this time.' Her aunt wore a slightly worried, hesitant expression. 'The project I told you about didn't go through.'

Jia Jia was ready with her next question when Leo gave an excuse and said that he really had to leave. He gathered his coat and wallet while the women waited in silence, and walked out the door.

Jia Jia continued, 'But I thought you told me—'

'Who was the boy?' Her aunt sat down with a grin.

'Oh, Auntie, don't think that it's so easy to move on.'

'But you really should. Chen Hang was not good to you,' her aunt said. 'You know, I blame myself. As you were growing up, I should have told you how important it is to love bravely. I should never have told you that you were too young to be dating that boy, what was his name again?'

'That boy from high school? Oh, please, don't expect me to remember!' They both laughed.

'Sometimes,' her aunt continued, 'we don't ask for things because we don't want to be broken. But that's how we drive away the life we care about. Maybe it's better to be more like your mother. No, no, don't object. She was broken, yes, but she knew what she wanted all along.'

In Jia Jia's memory of her mother's later years, she always had a glow of sadness around her. When her father fell in love with the other woman, Jia Jia saw her shattering like antique porcelain. Unable to separate herself from her mother's pain, she had concluded that love was the most fragile of bases for relationships: there had to be something else, some more rational reason for two people to be together, so that there could be a piece of solid ground to stand on when everything else crumbled. But what was she to think about her opinions now? Now that Chen Hang was gone, was her ground not collapsing, her life not broken?

'How are you getting used to living here by yourself?' Her aunt started fumbling through her handbag.

'Not too badly.'

'Oh, here it is! Li Chang's found you a job.' Her aunt picked out a business card and set it on the table. 'This is a friend of his. She wants someone to paint a Buddha on her wall.'

Jia Jia thought that there were professionals who specialised in religious paintings. Was it even acceptable for a non-religious person to be painting the Buddha?

'Auntie, I've never painted on a wall in my life. If she wants a painting to decorate her home, I can find—'

'I'm sure you'll be able to impress her.' She pointed at the horse painting. 'Look at how nice this is!'

Jia Jia picked up the card and studied it. The woman seemed to be a comedy film editor at a company she did not recognise. What an oddly specific profession, Jia Jia thought, she only edits comedies? There was a mobile number and a personal email. Jia Jia said that she would try to contact her. Her aunt, seemingly satisfied with Jia Jia's promise, rose and danced out the door, waving her hand behind her.

The comedy editor's name was Wan Lian, or Ms Wan, as Jia Jia would address her. She lived with her family in a duplex apartment in Yayuncun, further out from the centre. When Jia Jia visited the following Wednesday, Ms Wan was at home alone with a maid who was busy transferring bottles of imported beer from a box into the fridge.

'My husband is at work,' Ms Wan told Jia Jia.

Ms Wan was a few years older than Jia Jia. From the photos on the bookshelf, Jia Jia gathered that she had two children: one boy and one girl. The woman was incredibly small and bony, which made her head with her bob haircut appear overly large and round, like one of those bobble-head toys that people kept in cars. Her body looked so fragile that Jia Jia wondered how she had been able to give birth to two seemingly normal-sized children. When she carried a pot of hot water from the kitchen into the living room, Jia Jia watched her carefully, concerned that the large iron kettle might break her.

'So you see –' Ms Wan set the kettle on the table, dumped herself down on the sofa, and pointed to an empty white wall in the entrance hall – 'I'm thinking of having a Thangka painted on that wall.'

'I don't have any experience painting on silk appliqué.'

'Oh, no, not silk. I want the picture to be painted directly on the wall. I think that'd look nicer, wouldn't it?'

Jia Jia wanted to explain to this woman that Thangkas are normally painted and embroidered on silk. When Jia Jia was young, her mother had received a Thangka as a present from a Tibetan monk. She had studied it carefully every day after school – it was an incredibly intricate craft that took years of training to master. But Ms Wan cared little about what Jia Jia had to say and continued insisting that she thought a painting on the wall would be more beautiful.

'Ms Wan, may I ask, are you a Buddhist?'

'I believe in karma,' she responded. 'What do you think? Would you like to help me out?'

Jia Jia agreed and said that she would try her best. If it did not turn out well, she would not charge Ms

Wan any money. Ms Wan seemed to be pleased with the deal, and they settled on a final price of twenty thousand yuan.

Jia Jia painted in Ms Wan's home five days a week. Ms Wan insisted that she stay for dinner every time. The children would return from school and join them, but Jia Jia did not meet Ms Wan's husband until two weeks into the project – by which time she had begun to think that either the man returned home very late every night or did not return at all. One afternoon he pushed open the front door and seemed startled to see Jia Jia standing there, painting on his wall. He had a large beard, his hair had a few strands of grey and was tied up in a high ponytail. They exchanged a few words and Jia Jia found out that he owned a jazz lounge.

'I know that place,' Jia Jia said. 'I used to go there when it first opened. I was still an art student.'

'I'm glad to hear that,' he said in a soft and raspy voice. 'What are you painting here?'

'Your wife asked me to paint Shakyamuni here.'

He seemed to be completely unaware of what was going on in the household. Jia Jia pointed at the centre of the wall, above a pencilled outline of a lotus. 'It's more difficult than I had thought. I want to do it well.'

'That's wonderful. Don't let me disturb you.'

That was their only exchange. She left early that afternoon so that the husband and wife could spend some time together. No one told her to leave and the couple did not seem to mind her presence, but she did not feel like painting any more. Instead, she found herself heading to Leo's bar.

'I'm not sure about this job,' Jia Jia told Leo, as he watched her sit down on her stool. 'I barely have time to work on my own art.'

Leo took a glass and poured her some water. It seemed like she had decided to keep her hair down permanently. She looked exhausted, though also younger. Perhaps it was the way she was dressed – blue jeans, black sweater and white trainers. She had a canvas bag with her tools inside. Her lower eye make-up was a little smudged. Leo found her to be more beautiful this way. More honest, perhaps.

'I can't do it,' she repeated. 'How are we supposed to know what the Buddha looks like? What if the lotus is supposed to have, say, six petals instead of five? Then I would have messed it up.'

'I thought Buddhist wall paintings were only seen in caves and temples,' Leo said. 'This woman must be a devoted believer.'

'You know what?' Jia Jia pushed aside a small plate of olives and leaned across the counter closer to Leo. 'Yesterday when Ms Wan was studying the painting, she said to me, "I pray to this wall every night. I've been doing it ever since the first day you started working on it. I can't stop now." Then she said that it's the only way to make herself feel safe. *Every* night, this woman prays to my painting to feel safe ... and I barely even know what I'm doing.'

'Look at that guy.' Leo pointed out the window towards a guard dressed in uniform who was sitting at the entrance to the car park. 'Do you think he knows what he's doing?'

The boy was no more than eighteen years old. Indeed, it did not seem like he had had a proper education in safeguarding car parks. He saluted each driver with his left hand and his mouth opened slightly whenever an expensive model drove by.

'Don't be ridiculous, it's not the same.' Jia Jia laughed. Her slightly bulged teeth made her adorable.

'Well, sometimes I barely know what drink I'm making.'

'Is that so?'

Leo put his index finger on his lips, indicating that it was a secret not to be shared with other customers.

'What are your plans for Chinese New Year?' he asked, beginning to carve out an ice ball with a knife. 'Want to come with me to my parents'?'

Jia Jia's expression stiffened.

'I'll have to check with my family,' she said, averting her eyes. 'Hold on a minute.'

Pretending to make a phone call, Jia Jia stepped out of the bar and looked in the direction of the car park. The guard was playing on his phone when a red Porsche Panamera stopped at the barrier. The car honked, startling the boy, and he walked up to the window and said something to the driver with a nervous questioning expression on his face. Whatever the boy said seemed to have angered the driver and he started driving slowly towards the barrier. The boy panicked and slapped his hand on the door of the car.

'You fucking idiot!' Jia Jia heard the driver yell from his car.

Jia Jia walked around the corner of the building into the silent shadows. She allowed herself a crazy thought, one that involved starting a life with Leo, learning to love him – not the violent seas of love that she had read about in novels, but more a serene lake, contained within its boundaries. And she would bury Chen Hang away, sell the apartment, forget about the fish-man, tear up the drawing. Could she really live like that? No. Probably not. There was something unfulfilled about her relationship with Leo. The closer they pulled themselves together, the tighter her skin held her heart captive, unable to touch his. Still, she wanted to try, to free herself from Chen Hang, to try and live another kind of life.

By the time Jia Jia made her way back to the bar, the red Porsche was gone, and the boy sat there on his chair without his phone, turning his head to follow every car that passed by on the road.

At the end of the night, before the bar closed, Jia Jia accepted Leo's invitation.

6

Jia Jia had agreed to meet Leo in the afternoon to drive together to his parents'. She felt unsure and anxious. Three months after her husband's death, she was already spending the holidays with another man's family: maybe Chen Hang's parents were right, she thought, she was a curse. A destructive, vile scourge. First her mother, then her husband. And now, all tangled up with another man so soon, like moss that clings to other plants for life.

It was still early, not even lunchtime. Jia Jia checked her bank account, though she already knew how much was in there – forty thousand left from Chen Hang, plus ten thousand from Ms Wan as a deposit for the wall painting. She had to go shopping before meeting up with Leo: she could not arrive at his parents' door empty-handed. She might as well slap him across the face.

She put on a long, orange wool dress, tied her hair in a high ponytail, and rubbed some perfume on her wrists. She looked younger this way. Pleased with her appearance, she took the subway to SKP Mall and began browsing the shops. International brands lined the floors, and their windows were mopped so clean that there seemed almost no point in having them at all. Since the last time she had come here, a week or so before Chen Hang died, a few shops had moved from one floor, one corner, to another, like a pack of cards that had been shuffled.

Before Jia Jia and Chen Hang got married, he had taken her back to Fujian once to meet his parents. She had come to this mall then and selected some clothes for his mother and a watch for his father. Chen Hang had paid for it all. The watch shop was still there, but an ostentatious style with diamonds around the face had taken over the window display. Jia Jia stopped briefly to look at it and then walked past the black marble shopfront towards a section of the mall where she knew she would find cashmere. She flipped through the racks and picked out two matching red sweaters. The saleswoman told her the price: a little over seven thousand yuan for both.

'There is a holiday discount of forty per cent,' the saleswoman told her.

'How much will it be after the discount?' asked Jia Jia.

'The price I gave you was already inclusive of the discount, ma'am.' The saleswoman smiled and blinked at Jia Jia with lashes that were far too perfectly black and lush to be her own.

'That's right,' Jia Jia said, forcing a smile back at her. 'I'll take another look around.'

Jia Jia quickly left the mall, feeling like a rat that had been caught stealing. She had intentionally chosen to shop in the section where the brands were cheaper, but those sweaters alone would have cost her almost two months of apartment charges. They were marvellous sweaters, though, soft and fine; she would very much have liked to buy one for herself. But she was still living in the apartment that was far too costly, with a job that could hardly be considered a job. She entered the subway without looking back, feeling the cashmere saleswoman's fake eyelashes flickering at her from behind.

Jia Jia got off at Dongdaqiao station and marched purposefully into Blue Island Mall. Shoppers dressed in all kinds of bright colours crowded the floors, digging through piles of clothes and trying out skincare products. This mall was far too hot despite it being near freezing outside. Almost all the salespeople were middle-aged women. A few of them stood next to a cashier, chatting about their children while buttoning shirts and folding them back into semi-neat piles of squares. Jia Jia roamed the various floors, searching for knitwear shops. She had decided, for no particular reason, that she was going to buy Leo's parents matching sweaters. Finally, she came across a brand that seemed promising.

The wool felt surprisingly soft in her hands. All she needed to do now was find two styles that could be gifted as a pair. She examined the racks, making sure not to leave a single piece unseen. She came across a dolphin-grey crewneck sweater, with flowers embroidered on each of the shoulders. She called the saleswoman over.

A plump woman with a pixie haircut approached her. She had a large black mole on her face right next to her nose that startled Jia Jia when she turned her head.

'You want this sweater?' Mole-lady asked.

'I wanted to see if there are any men's sweaters in the same colour,' Jia Jia said quietly, afraid to irritate this woman.

Mole-lady bent over, grunting, and took out a pile of folded sweaters from some low drawers. As she straightened up and dumped the pile onto a table, her body emanated a strong smell of tobacco combined with sweat.

'Check here,' Mole-lady said.

Jia Jia compared the sweaters to the one in her hand. Towards the bottom, she found one that was in the same shade of grey, with a black horizontal stripe across the chest. This could certainly do, she thought.

'How much are the two?' Jia Jia asked.

'This one is ...' Mole-lady lifted her head and checked the price for the women's one, squinting her eyes at the tag. 'One thousand eight hundred and ten yuan. And the other one is a bit less, if I remember correctly. Let me see ... it's one thousand six hundred and ten.'

'Are there any discounts? It's a present. I imagine you'd have some sales going on at this time of the year. Could you give me a member's discount or something?'

'Are you a member?' Mole-lady looked up at Jia Jia, displeased.

'No, I'm not. But I could apply—'

Another group of customers walked in and Mole-lady immediately left Jia Jia to greet them.

'What were you saying?' she asked when she returned.

'I said that I could apply for a membership.'

'We don't do member discounts.' Mole-lady began folding the sweaters.

'Then why did you ask me if I was a member? But never mind, can I buy both for three thousand?'

'Young lady, this is a mall and we are a brand, we don't bargain here. If you can't afford it, go to another shop.' Mole-lady took the grey sweaters and began stuffing them back into the drawers.

Jia Jia took a few deep breaths, summoning all the patience in her.

'... dressed nicely like a rich girl,' mumbled the woman to herself. 'The bag is probably fake. If you don't have money, don't come out shopping.'

Jia Jia wanted to file a complaint with the manager, but found she could not piece together the words in her mouth. She was not good at this, too accustomed to being with Chen Hang, who would have demanded to speak to a supervisor right at the beginning when he first sensed the woman's attitude. And Jia Jia, of course, would have assumed the role of the silent wife.

She turned and fled the mall, more wretched than before. A rat that had not only been caught, but beaten up, stamped on, driven into a dark corner. She felt herself shrinking, her back curving, her muscles weakening. She hailed a taxi.

'SKP Mall,' she said to the driver. She had to save herself, to charge out of the corner and make the grandest appearance on a bigger, open stage.

When they arrived, Jia Jia paid the driver and told him to keep the change. She stormed past the European designers, the jewellery stores, the watch brands, and approached the young woman with the fake eyelashes.

'I would like the two red sweaters that I picked out before,' Jia Jia said, as calmly and firmly as she could.

The saleswoman blinked, and then smiled courteously. 'Certainly,' she responded. 'Anything else you'd like?'

'That's it,' Jia Jia said. 'Wait a minute, give me this scarf too.' She took a red scarf from the rack and waved it at her.

After the woman had gone behind a door to gather the items, Jia Jia felt able to breathe again, having picked up a piece of her dignity. The woman wrapped the items carefully and rang up the total. Jia Jia paid, shopped around inside the mall a bit longer, bought nothing more, and went out.

She sat on a bench, the shopping bag lying flat on her lap. She wanted to cry, but she did not have time to go home and re-do her make-up before meeting Leo. So she held her face in her hands and imagined herself crying, screaming at the city, screaming so hard that her heart was coming out and everybody could hear her. She imagined herself crying like a newborn, innocent of all the twists and turns of being alive, the crossroads, the dead ends. She imagined herself crying for only a short while, before she stood up and walked down into the subway to catch the next onward train.

Jia Jia would be the second woman that Leo had ever taken to see his parents. The last time had been five years ago. He wanted them to accept her, and more importantly, he hoped that she would like them. But immediately after he had asked her to spend the holidays with him, he had regretted his words, expecting her to refuse. He should have been more cautious about throwing the question at her like that. Her acceptance had been worried and guarded, as if he had left her with no choice, and to reject his invitation would have been an act of rudeness. From what Leo had learned so far about Jia Jia, he knew that she always chose the option that she thought made others happy, not what brought happiness to herself. So Jia Jia had agreed, and ever since then, Leo had seen an unconcealable although well-hidden trace of anxiety in her. She had sent him messages often, enquiring about what his parents liked to eat; what kind of alcohol they preferred; whether his father smoked Chinese cigarettes or imported ones; what his parents' shirt sizes were.

On New Year's Eve, she turned up at his compound's car park a little before four o'clock. Leo was not a car person; he was aware that there was nothing impressive about his car, a regular black Honda Accord. He had considered taking a taxi with Jia Jia, but ultimately decided that he would drive. This was him. He was not Chen Hang. He wanted her to see that.

She had bought his parents matching red cashmere sweaters, she told Leo in the car, each a size larger than their usual sizes, reasoning that this way, they could wear layers underneath during the cold winters. She had also bought a red scarf for his mother and some Yuxi cigarettes for his father.

It was the best time of the year to be in Beijing. People withdrew into their homes and settled in circles around their living-room tables; the women making flawlessly arranged rows of dumplings, the men chatting over cups of tea and puffs of smoke about all the events that had taken place during the past year. Although Leo never left the city during Chinese New Year, he had not spent the holidays at home for two years now. His parents had not insisted either – they believed that he had been busy with work. He had a close relationship with his family, but he relished his peaceful solitude more, going on hikes at Fragrant Hills, riding a bike down Changan Avenue, and even journeying on the empty subways, which became much more enjoyable without the usual migrant workers racing to their destinations.

Leo's father was a researcher at the health and science department of Peking University. He was a forward-thinking scholar who spent his days either working in his lab, teaching, or reading at home with a cigarette in his hand. Leo's parents' apartment was not very big, but his father had converted the second room into a study where he could read and write. He

was writing a book. He had been working on it for as
long as Leo could remember. He made it a point to
spend some time in his study every night before he
went to bed, either reading or writing. Often, Leo's
mother would find him asleep in his armchair with a
book opened to the first few pages.

Leo drove fast on the empty roads and they arrived
at his parents' without any delays. They lived in the
north-west area of Beijing, just outside the second
ring road. When his mother opened the door, Leo
started to see what he had foisted upon Jia Jia. His
mother was wearing a decade-old apron that was
stained all over and was wiping her hands on it.

'Sorry,' she said as she invited them in, smiling
embarrassedly while patting Jia Jia on the shoulder.
'I'll be a little busy in the kitchen. Go and chat with
your father! He's been talking about you for weeks.'

'Can I help you in the kitchen?' Jia Jia asked.

'Oh, don't worry, please, go, go with him.' Leo's
mother pointed towards the living room. 'It's faster if
I do it alone,' she added. She began rolling dough with
one hand while waving the other in the air.

'Jia Jia, don't bother,' Leo said. 'Come.'

'Yes, yes, come!' his father echoed deep and loud
from the living room.

Jia Jia handed the gifts to Leo's father and explained
what she had got for the couple. Leo watched his
father nod and thank her. He left the sweaters

untouched in the bag and pulled out the cigarettes to examine the carton.

'I should really stop smoking,' he said. 'A colleague of mine found polyps in his intestines during his annual check-up and had to have them taken out. We're getting old, son.' He looked at Leo and sighed. 'But I suppose giving up now isn't going to make such a big difference.'

Jia Jia smiled and faintly shook her head.

The sun seeped through the drying laundry at the window and cast its beams on Jia Jia when she sat down on the sofa. She looked like an old photograph, Leo thought, gentle and delicate. At that moment he felt proud of the cleanness in her beauty – her pale skin and minimal make-up. His father had always proclaimed that he did not care about how much housework a woman could do but she must have a pure heart.

There was something particularly moving about the way Jia Jia interacted with his father, Leo thought. There was a sense of distanced familiarity, as if she were a close friend from long ago. She did not speak much, but she seemed to be at ease listening to him blabber on about the different illnesses that were tor-menting his colleagues and friends. And occasion-ally, when silence reigned, she would take a sip of her tea or ask a question, encouraging his father to talk more.

'One day last month,' his father said, 'it was sunny, so I was with our neighbour in the park. You know, the other professor who lives two floors up?' He turned to Leo and then back to Jia Jia. 'He brought a friend,' he continued. 'An old man with sunglasses and a walking stick.'

'Poor man,' Jia Jia said, appearing genuinely regretful.

'He also had the newspaper in his hands,' Leo's father said.

'But I thought he was blind?' Leo said.

'I still don't know whether he was blind or not. I never managed to ask him,' his father said.

'We think that he was so used to reading the papers every day that even when he became blind he couldn't stop,' Leo's mother said as she plodded into the living room.

'Ma.' Leo stood up and guided his mother to the sofa. 'Come, take your apron off and rest for a bit with us.'

'Oh! Jia Jia, you brought presents?' asked his mum. 'We really don't need anything.'

Jia Jia offered her the sweater and the scarf. Leo's mother immediately took them out of the bag and held them up against the sun.

'This must be expensive! It's so soft! We really don't need anything. Next time, don't bother buying us presents, just bring our son back more often!' His mother laughed and examined the scarf again.

'I saw the blind man a few times again in the park,' his father continued, reaching out and gently brushing his wife out of his way so that he could look at Leo. 'He would always be with another person, always someone different. Then he stopped turning up. We thought that the man must have got ill, or even died. Later we heard that his children sold his place and checked him into a retirement home.'

'Heartless!' Leo's mother added. 'To lose your home when you're old ...'

As if she could not bear the sadness of the conversation, she left to return to the kitchen, apron still tied to her waist.

Dinner was simple. They were the kind of family who would not cook anything special for the festival. Still, it was a big meal, with two meat and two vegetable dishes, along with a soup. Usually, Leo's parents would only have one dish for dinner, and never more than two, for fear of wasting food. His father did not like to eat leftovers, so if they did not finish this meal, his mother would be eating the rest of it for the next three days, steaming and re-steaming the food until either she had eaten everything or it had disintegrated into a pile of inedible mush.

'Are you living with your family?' Leo's mother asked Jia Jia at the dinner table.

'I live in an apartment by myself. Near his bar.' She turned her head briefly and smiled at Leo.

'Rent must be high over in that area,' his father noted.

'Thankfully, I own the apartment,' Jia Jia said.

Leo's parents were surprised. They both, as if rehearsed, put down their bowls and looked at Jia Jia, waiting for her to elaborate.

'It is my husband's apartment. He's gone now,' Jia Jia said, mirroring his parents' actions and setting her own bowl on the table.

'Oh,' Leo's mother said abruptly.

'I see,' said his father, hastening with the game expression Leo had seen so many times. 'We don't mind at all. Not only you young people, but my wife and I are also part of the modern generation.'

Leo's mother reverted her gaze to her chopsticks and resumed eating in silence. Jia Jia's phone rang. She rushed to the living room and muted it. When she returned, Leo continued the conversation.

'We met at my bar,' said Leo.

'Have you met her ex-husband too, then?' his father asked.

'Yes, he has,' Jia Jia responded.

Again, almost in sync, both Leo's parents leaned back in their chairs. The table fell silent for a moment, and his father's eyebrows contracted, as if he was trying to crack a difficult problem.

'Must have been a decent man to find a good girl like yourself,' he finally said, giving a forced smile. Leo's mother nodded.

Leo took a deep breath. He was relieved that his parents were processing the news of Jia Jia's previous marriage, and surprisingly well. It was not them, he told himself, but the generation before theirs that stuck to their feudal ways of thinking. He was astounded by how swiftly his parents seemed to have adapted, how their principles were edging away from the conservative, the outdated. He felt proud of his scholarly parents for their tolerance.

After dinner, Leo told Jia Jia that he wanted to stay to wait for the New Year countdown.

'Have you been to Europe? Or America?' Leo's father asked Jia Jia as he stored his new carton of cigarettes in the drawer beneath the television.

'I used to visit Europe quite often with my husband,' Jia Jia said. 'Mostly France and Italy. But I've only been to America once. I prefer Europe – the museums and art galleries are always inspiring.'

'Are people afraid there?' asked his father. 'I mean, of terrorism, like all these attacks I'm hearing of. I get the feeling that Europeans just go on with their lives.'

'I'm not sure, I don't think—'

Leo's father yelled to his wife: 'Stop doing stuff, come and join the children for a bit! Bring the snacks

Old Li gave us!' He spun back to face Leo and Jia Jia.
'My friend brought some snacks back from England. I
remember when we first went to London, a long time
ago, we were such idiots back then. We were poor,
those days we had it much worse, so you're lucky.
When we saw tinned pet food, we thought those were
cans of dog- and cat-meat. It was the cheapest food so
that's what we ate! Oh, it was disgusting. And who
would've thought that British people sold pet food in
supermarkets!' His father laughed, briefly choking on
his own saliva.

Leo's mother, having wrapped all the food with
plastic and left it out to cool, finally reappeared in the
living room and joined the conversation.

'Come, I was telling them about our trip to London
years ago,' Leo's father told his wife, still coughing.

'Oh, yes, yes, we didn't have the same privileges you
have nowadays.'

'My mother used to tell me similar stories as well,'
Jia Jia said with a smile on her face.

Jia Jia had never mentioned her parents to Leo. He
studied her as she started talking about her mother
travelling to Xi'an, to Guizhou, to Chengdu in the
eighties. She wore a sombre expression, eyes a little
watery like white jade. From the way she told the
stories it seemed as though the memories of her
mother were fractional and incomplete, but she
recounted her experiences without a single mention

of her father. Sometimes she paused, looking about the room, as if questioning the accuracy of her recollections.

As Jia Jia spoke, a feeling began to descend on Leo with the relentlessness of June rains. He was now the outsider at this gathering, unable to interrupt the conversation. Why was she sharing so much with his parents? Why was she going on and on, story after story, like an enthusiastic busker narrating tales to children? Jia Jia kept telling the stories, way out of her usual character, in dramatic waves of joy and grief.

And then she was telling them that her husband died three months ago. Leo watched as his parents lost their smiles, and exchanged an unsubtle look of shock. The topic had come up when his mother asked Jia Jia who she had travelled with on her last trip to France, whether it had been her mother or her husband.

'My husband,' Jia Jia responded. 'That was our last trip together. We were supposed to go to Sanya last year, but he died.'

'What happened?' his mother asked, gasping.

Jia Jia shook her head. 'I'm not sure.'

Leo observed his parents cautiously, trying to decipher their reactions to another piece of unexpected news. But the pair sat in silence frowning down at the pile of British snacks.

Jia Jia's phone rang again.

'It's my aunt,' she told Leo. 'Probably calling to send her holiday greetings.'

As Jia Jia stood, Leo's parents looked up from the sofa and forced an awkward smile. His mother kept fidgeting with her sleeves. Jia Jia excused herself and stepped outside the apartment.

'Son,' his father said when the door had clicked shut. He rubbed his knees, straightened his posture, and took a deep breath. 'A widow is bad luck.'

'Your father is right,' his mother said.

'That's outdated thinking,' Leo said.

'I've seen some women from my home town who married two or three men who all died within a few years. Some women just bring bad luck to men,' his father said.

'Ba, you're a scientist.'

'She's a great girl, but this ...' his mother muttered, tapping her hands on her knees. 'What a New Year ...'

'You're our only son,' his father said. 'Have you ever noticed that some people just have negativity around them? All their friends and circles have misfortunes. Ever noticed that?'

Leo argued. His parents fought back. Leo became angrier, and found himself raising his voice for the first time in years. This might have been another reason why he had avoided coming home. He was wrong. What kind of unrealistic expectations had he brought with him here today? His parents were at an age where they had become stubborn, and no matter how forward-thinking they might have been ten, twenty years ago, now they were too proud and old-fashioned even to link their bank accounts to their phone apps for fear of their money being stolen. Too set in their own ways to turn on the air purifier that Leo had bought them, throwing their windows open every day to let in what they still believed to be 'fresh air'.

Jia Jia returned, and as she strode into the room, bringing a gust of cold with her, the family stopped quarrelling. Leo could tell that Jia Jia had something on her mind, just as she could most likely sense the tense atmosphere around the tea table.

'Let's go,' Leo said, grabbing their coats.

'But it's only ten—' his mother began.

'Take some snacks with you,' his father said.

But Leo had stopped listening and stormed out, holding Jia Jia's wrists and squeezing them too hard.

In the car, Leo asked Jia Jia what her phone call had been about.

'Things are a bit complicated,' Jia Jia said.

'What things?'

'I'm just a bit worried,' she said, refusing to look at him.

'Yes, I can tell, but what happened?'

'I'll have to see my aunt soon. Don't worry about it.'

'For Christ's sake!' He gripped the wheel hard with both hands. 'I've asked you three times already, just answer my question.'

'Why are you angry?' Jia Jia sat up from the seat and turned to face him. Her voice was loud. 'Because I told your parents about Chen Hang? Should I be ashamed about my husband's death? Should I feel sorry for ruining your family gathering? This is who I am, and to be with me, you'll have to accept the fact that I'm a widow.'

'We could've told them at another time.' He took a deep breath.

'So you are ashamed—'

'No.'

'Don't you lie to me.'

Jia Jia glared at him. He stared straight ahead. From the corner of his eye, he could see that the New Year's fireworks flecked her face in different colours, making her look as if she had scales on her cheeks. Her hair was falling loose. She kept her eyes locked on him, and Leo sensed a resolve in her that he had not seen before. She had never looked at him like that; her glances had always been fleeting. At times, she would be playful, or sensual, and at other times, she would be distant and elusive. But here in the car, watching him, she had her mind set on something.

It was the first time that she had told him what she wanted from him. *Don't lie to me.*

But he could not give her the truth that she demanded. He asked himself whether he was indeed embarrassed about bringing home a woman whom he knew, deep inside, his parents would not accept. While he drove past all the bright apartments and the dark offices, he thought about how much he wanted to crack open her defences as she sat there next to him, to learn about her insecurities. This woman whose past he barely knew anything about.

'You've never told me those stories about your mother,' he said.

'What's the point of talking about those who are not around any more?'

'I just want to understand you better, Jia Jia, to know how you're feeling. I don't know who you are.' His voice filled the car and rang in his own ears. 'You won't let me know who you are.'

She turned and looked out the window at the fireworks, and for a moment those muted explosions were the only sounds.

'How can you really know someone?' she said finally. 'Even if I take my heart out, dissect it into pieces, and explain each piece in intricate detail to you – in the end, I would still have to stuff the whole damn thing back into my own chest.'

For the rest of the journey back, they remained silent. Once, near Dongzhimen, Leo had to brake suddenly as a child ran out across the street. He dropped

Jia Jia off in front of her apartment. She smiled at him before getting out of his car. It was a regretful, tender and sad smile.

She drew her coat tight, walked towards the building, and did not look back.

7

While Jia Jia was on the phone outside Leo's parents' apartment, her aunt had told her that Li Chang had been detained on charges of bribery. He had gifted a sum of cash along with a work of calligraphy to a government official and benefited from a business opportunity in exchange. The official had been put under investigation, and Li Chang, along with numerous other businessmen, had been arrested.

In the subsequent weeks, her aunt lost her brightness and became afraid of almost everything. Many nights, she stayed at Jia Jia's apartment. She met everyone she could find who had connections with the Disciplinary Committee, but most of them did not have any valuable information, and others only provided false comfort.

Eventually, Jia Jia's aunt started distracting herself by taking classes in flower arrangement. She was very thin, and the skin on the back of her neck draped loosely over the pure gold chain that she always wore. She was tired all the time. Jia Jia urged her to see a doctor; she agreed, but would always find a different excuse to cancel the appointment. She either slept all day or did not sleep at all. She also started smoking, and her arguments with Jia Jia's grandmother became more frequent.

March turned to April and Jia Jia had still not seen Leo. She had not gone to his bar, and he had not contacted her either. Instead, Jia Jia focused her attention on completing her commission. (*Be wary when interacting with Ms Wan and don't speak too much about Li Chang*, her aunt had told her.) Originally, she had only been asked to paint the middle section of the wall, leaving two wide strips of white on each side, but Ms Wan was so captivated by her work that she extended her commission to have the side sections filled as well. She agreed to pay Jia Jia an extra ten thousand yuan for it.

'Take your time,' Ms Wan told her. 'Fine products come from slow work.'

'You seem to be at home quite often these days – has business been quiet?' Jia Jia asked as she started sketching on the white wall, extending the blue pond outwards.

'I'm fed up. I decided to take a break.'

Ms Wan took off her reading glasses and set her copy of *Meditations* down on the table. 'The film industry is hopeless,' she said.

'I haven't seen a good movie for a long time,' Jia Jia said.

Ms Wan pointed the remote control at the television. 'Look at these two guys in this new drama. They look the same! Same haircut, same face shape, same build. How is the audience supposed to know which one is which?'

Jia Jia directed her attention to the screen. Another drama about the struggles between the Red Army and the Nationalist Party. The main character, a spy for the Red Army, was a tall man with dark eyebrows. Indeed, he looked very much like the captain in the Nationalist Army. She imagined the action scenes, one man fighting against his own shadow.

'There is a lot of money,' Ms Wan said regretfully. 'And the government is supportive of cultural activities, which is great, they say. But I'm so tired of making bad films. Do you want to have a drink with me?'

Ms Wan reached into a cupboard, picked out a half-finished bottle of port and filled two glasses. Jia Jia watched her carefully as she held the bottle, her wrists shaking as she poured, her big head crooking to one side.

'The uneducated are becoming better and better off in this country,' she said as she slowly returned to Jia Jia with a glass of wine. 'Good movies don't make big money any more.'

She handed the drink to Jia Jia, tottered back to the sofa, put on her glasses and went on with her reading.

*

Jia Jia stayed late that day. Ms Wan put the children to bed, called the driver, and was whisked off to her husband's jazz lounge close to midnight. Jia Jia continued painting in silence by the light of a single lamp.

A little past two a.m., she felt tired and took a break. She had not touched the port, but now she picked up the glass and stood back from the wall. The immense project had become wondrous. The ancient Buddha Shakyamuni sat on a lotus flower in the middle, holding a beggar's bowl in his left hand and calling the earth as witness with his right. The rest of the piece depicted the major events in the life of the Buddha. Jia Jia had painted it in sophisticated detail, mostly gold and orange tones, occasionally sprinkling splashes of emerald or cobalt for clothes or bodies of water.

As Jia Jia gazed at the painting in the dim yellow light, the rings in the blue pond rippled and the water began seeping out, covering the entire wall. The demons, gods, and eventually the ancient Buddha himself, were submerged until all that appeared in front of Jia Jia was a single fish, silver like a coin.

She had no doubt that it was the same creature she had seen before, but larger and tougher this time. It swam in circles, as if shaken by something. The body of water, as deep as ever, churned and threatened to sink everything in its path. Instinctively, Jia Jia took a step backwards, but stopped as the fish turned to face her, inviting her to step into the water.

The air had turned cold.

Jia Jia reached out cautiously and stroked the creature's tail. Startled, it shook her hand off and continued swimming. The scales on its body were in large diamond shapes, glistening and pristine. She tried to find similarities between the fish in front of her and the fish-man Chen Hang had sketched, but there were none. The shapes were different.

Still hesitant, Jia Jia dropped her wine glass and walked forward into what used to be her wall painting and was now only water, and tried to touch the fish again. This time, it turned its head towards Jia Jia's outstretched finger and lingered there for a moment. She dived into the water and swam towards the darkness; the fish followed her. As she went deeper, she noticed that it was glowing faintly, providing the only source of light in the abyss.

Once again, she lost sight of where she had come from. And there was no evidence that she was moving forward either; perhaps she was only treading water, kicking behind her, with the fish alongside. She turned around and tried to direct her body the other way, but she was not sure any more. The silver light from the fish dimmed and vanished, and Jia Jia was alone. Was she going to drown? Was she going to stay there and wait until she starved? What about the port? It must have stained the carpet. Was the floor carpeted? Jia Jia could not remember.

She closed her eyes and stopped moving.

Time passed and she heard a sound. She was leaning against the wall now. The solid surface felt like ice
against her back. Tears began running down her face,
warming her skin. The port was spilt on the marble
floor.

The door lock turned, and Ms Wan and her husband entered.

Seeing Jia Jia crying that night, Ms Wan had been
worried. Jia Jia assured her that she was simply moved
by the story of the Buddha.

'That, truly, is the power of religion,' Ms Wan noted
with profound compassion.

The next day, Jia Jia informed her real estate agent
that she wanted to move out of the apartment as soon
as possible. She felt liberated to find out that she did
not need to stay there to see the fish and the water. As
there had been no interested buyers since December,
she said that she would not mind letting it at a low-
er-than-market rate if that was easier. According to
the agent, it was better for Jia Jia to empty the apartment and move out before showing it to prospective
tenants and buyers.

'Many clients prefer homes that look newer and
unoccupied,' he told her.

Jia Jia's aunt helped her pack. Now that Li Chang
was not there, Jia Jia thought she could temporarily live

with her grandmother and aunt. She had been so adamant about the move that her aunt had made no objections; perhaps she had also been feeling worried about leaving the old woman alone so often. By this time, her aunt had begun to avoid the subject of Li Chang entirely when she was staying with her niece. She would wait until she thought Jia Jia was asleep before whispering into the phone for hours with her friends. Jia Jia never probed; without Chen Hang's connections, there was nothing that she could do to help. In fact, when the government's anti-corruption efforts had begun a few years earlier, Jia Jia had been fearful for her own husband's safety. Once, while she and Chen Hang were watching the morning news together, Jia Jia had made a casual, sympathetic comment about the corrupt businessmen and their families who had been forced to flee the country with their money.

'No need for you to worry about such things,' Chen Hang had told her. 'I'm not an idiot like those people.'

She recalled, though, that Chen Hang had often come and gone with boxes of expensive wines or wild ginseng in the boot of his car. Last New Year's, he had pulled out a thick crisp pile of one-hundred-yuan notes from an envelope and handed it to her, saying that it was red pocket money from a friend. She had bought a sculpture at auction with the money. It was a piece of dark green marble carved into a cubist-style figure of a woman; long and thin, with her hips slightly pointed towards the left side. The night after she brought it home, Chen Hang had not returned until the early hours. She had drunk three espressos and stayed awake past midnight, then applied a thin layer of foundation to her face and on her kite-shaped birthmark, and sat on the sofa in her black silk dress, next to her new art piece, waiting for her husband. By the time he came back, she had fallen asleep.

While Jia Jia was packing, she glanced at the sculpture forsaken in the corner of the room, trying to decide whether it belonged to her. She did not want to bring any of Chen Hang's possessions with her, but she folded everything and stored it all in boxes anyway. She collected together the unfinished bottles of cognac; drank some and poured out the rest, watching the brown liquid drain down the kitchen sink. She stripped the sheets off the bed and thought that she had never seen anything so desolate as a naked mattress. She could hardly remember what it was like, sleeping next to Chen Hang in this bed. Since the second year of their marriage, she had often gone to sleep alone, her husband returning late and drunk and falling asleep on the sofa still wearing his coat. Sometimes, he did not turn up until the next morning, and would quickly shower and change before heading out to the office again. After the sculpture incident, Jia Jia had stopped staying up at all to wait for his return. She gave one last look at the piece, auctioned at a high price only to end up in an abandoned apartment, carrying no sentiment, far removed from its creator. Perhaps it deserved a better owner, she thought, before dragging the last box out into the corridor and closing the door behind her.

She took all her own art and clothes with her and called a van to her grandmother's home. Chen Hang had been dead for six months, and her marriage was packed away in crates. From the van window, the streets appeared at once familiar and obscure. Looking up at the buildings, it seemed that the city she had known so well had been reshaped, rearranged somehow. Petrol fumes and the driver's smoky body odour wafted back at her. For a while, Jia Jia watched the hanging charm with its piece of amber sway from the rear-view mirror in irregular rhythms, in different directions. After they had zigzagged through the city's afternoon traffic and finally steered into the third ring road, Jia Jia took out her phone and dialled her father's number.

8

When the hired van pulled up at her grandmother's building, Jia Jia's friend Qing was sitting cross-legged on the front steps, waiting for her, an
unlit cigarette between her lips. She always rolled her
own cigarettes, a European habit that she had per-
fected during art school.

Jia Jia had few friends she kept in touch with from
those days, and Qing was one of them. Of the three
roommates from her first year, Jia Jia had become
closest with Qing. They had nothing in common
besides their passion for creating art, but back then,
that single commonality had been enough for them to
spend every day together, painting in silence, until the
sun had set and risen again.

Qing had short, dark brown hair that always smelt
like rushes. She claimed that she had kept the same
hairstyle her entire life, though it used to be black
when she was younger, and that the scent came from
the Japanese tatami bed that her mother had installed

in her room when she was a girl. Jia Jia admired Qing's
ability to stay true to herself, to have an identity and
one only. Qing's wardrobe was filled with olive-green
T-shirts and black jeans, and those things were all she
ever wore, except in the winter when she would put
on a black padded denim jacket.

Qing stuffed her cigarette behind her ear when she
saw Jia Jia.

'Qing's Home Movers reporting for duty!' She lifted
her right hand, holding the neon-green lighter to her
temple, and gave Jia Jia a salute.

They both laughed and proceeded to carry boxes
upstairs to the second floor. Every so often, Jia Jia's
grandmother stuck her head out from the kitchen
window and asked if they wanted pears.

By the time they had emptied everything from the
van, night had fallen, and Jia Jia's grandmother had
settled into a deep doze that would last until four in
the morning – the time she began cooking a pot of
plain breakfast congee. The plate of pears sat on the
bedside table waiting for Jia Jia and Qing.

Jia Jia's childhood bedroom had been converted
into a spare room. It was the only one that faced north
and overlooked the main road, making it much louder
than the others, which all faced the courtyard. The
white walls were yellowing and so were the curtains.
With the boxes piled on top of each other and filling
up the room, there was hardly anywhere to stand.

'Jia Jia, you have a lot of unpacking to do,' Qing said as she popped a half-moon of pear into her mouth and collapsed onto the single bed. The bed was made for Jia Jia already; the sheets were pale green and did not match with the purple-striped pillowcase.

'Also, about what you asked me last time,' Qing said. 'I heard back from a gallery who told me that they'd like to speak to you. Maybe you can organise a little exhibition or something.'

Jia Jia sat down next to Qing.

'I rang my father today,' Jia Jia said.

Qing sat up.

'I called him in the van,' Jia Jia continued. 'He suggested we meet for dinner. What's the gallery's name?'

'But you never call your dad.' Qing took a card out from her back pocket and handed it over. 'Here. They said that you can call in any time next week.'

'Thank you, Qing.' Jia Jia studied the card. She had never heard of the gallery before. 'So, are you still dating that guitarist?' she looked up and asked.

'What are these?' Qing started removing canvases from a box.

'Failed art. Are you still dating him? The tall guy with the purple guitar.'

'I'm thirty-one. I've decided that I need to consider my future a bit more, find someone more dependable.'

She held up one of Jia Jia's paintings. 'You haven't painted something so many times since university. A fish ... without a head?'

'There's supposed to be a man's head there.' Jia Jia pointed to the empty oval on the canvas. 'You know, Chen Hang was dependable.'

Moonlight shone in, revealing a thin layer of dust on top of everything: the television, the collectible book sets on the shelves, the ink painting of a red-crowned crane in the corner, the lantern hung on the window frame. Jia Jia recognised the lantern – it was one of the many things that had belonged to her mother and one of the few that were left. She had purchased it from a craftsman in Chongqing. Jia Jia's mother instilled stories into every object that she brought home with her from her travels. She asked young Jia Jia to guess where they came from and where they would go.

Wherever they go, it will be a better place, her mother once said.

Jia Jia ran her index finger along the edge of the lantern. Where *had* they gone? Where was the ceramic pot from Jingdezhen? The flute from Yuping? The bronze dragon from Xi'an? The qipao from Shanghai? The roll of embroidered fabric from Suzhou?

Did things disappear one by one, or altogether? she wondered. The past seemed to have become merely what remained.

'All these years, my father never married that new woman,' Jia Jia continued. 'Why do you think so?'

Qing shrugged. 'Maybe he doesn't want more family. I need a smoke.'

'Not here inside my grandma's apartment.' Jia Jia lightly punched Qing on the arm.

Perhaps Qing was right, Jia Jia thought, maybe he never wanted a new family. Now that she had lost her own, she seemed to understand her father a little, his unwillingness to start another family, to move on so completely. From the day he announced that he was in love again, to the moment he drove his car away with all his belongings, it was Jia Jia's mother who had been desperate to expel him from their home. Back when Jia Jia was a small child and morality was a more definite thing, she had chosen to stand with both feet on her mother's side, offering to her alone – the only victim in her mind – all the love that her young, delicate body could possibly summon. She had ignored, forgotten, those afternoons when she observed her father from the window of their apartment, pacing around, sometimes even knocking on their door. She had forgotten that she had never opened it for him, that she had deserted him too.

Qing stood and picked up her bag.

'Don't you want to eat something before you leave?' Jia Jia asked.

'Dieting!'

Qing took her cigarette from her ear, swung her bag behind her shoulder, and waved the hand that was holding the lighter. Jia Jia observed from her window as Qing exited the building and mounted her scooter. She shouted, 'Thank you,' as Qing disappeared around the corner, cigarette in her mouth.

A week after her move, Jia Jia was sitting at a small, round table with four chairs in a quiet corner of a Shanghainese restaurant. A waitress in a black skirt suit handed her a menu that felt as thick as a novel.

She was half an hour early and relieved to be away from her grandmother's for the first time since moving in. She had told Ms Wan that she was ill with a fever and could not finish the last section of the wall painting until she felt better. Instead, she had sat in her room and toiled over her own fish-man paintings in vain. The room was too small, too restricting. She did not remember it being that way. Every day, she felt as though she was in a tank of water, suffocating. Her aunt was rarely home, but in the dead of night, Jia Jia would hear her whispering and fighting with her grandmother about Li Chang.

Jia Jia studied the expertly-shot food photos inside the menu. She decided that she would begin her conversation with her father by complimenting the quality of the menu's paper – it felt like waxed cardboard. It would be an appropriate way to praise him for his restaurant choice, she thought. She had phoned her father from the van to tell him that she was moving out. Since then, she had realised that staying with her aunt and grandmother was not a long-term solution. They had developed their own way of living together through the years without her, and in the past few days, Jia Jia had felt out of place anywhere but in her own, tiny room.

She had not slept much the night before, unable to decide on what to say to her father, worrying over her decision to move into her grandmother's home. She imagined how cramped it would be after Li Chang came back. Should she ask to move into her father's place? He had a spacious three-bedroom apartment to himself. He was getting older, he would surely be pleased to have a daughter around to take care of him, to keep him company, to brew him some tea and chat with him at night. She had made up her mind that this time she was not going to get upset over his usual nonchalance. At the very least, she reasoned, she would have more space to work on her art if she lived with him.

She closed the menu, sipped on the Dragon Well tea that was brought to her, and waited for her father to arrive. An elderly, grey-haired couple was sitting at the table next to hers.

'I hit my arm on something sharp last night,' the old woman said. She looked like an older version of Ms

Wan – heavy head, bony body. Even her bob haircut was the same.

'Where?' the old man asked.

'In the bathroom.'

'Are you all right now?'

'I found a plaster.'

The waitress brought a plate of braised pork belly and carefully placed it between them. The old woman picked up a piece with her chopsticks and dropped it carefully onto the old man's rice. She then fetched another piece and stuffed it directly into her own mouth. They both chewed.

'It tastes good,' she said, munching open-mouthed with difficulty, revealing the few teeth she had left.

The old man nodded.

'Lunch was good yesterday,' she said.

'It was good to see the kids,' he said.

'Good, good,' she said.

They stopped talking and continued to eat. Their eyes were quiet, composed, without a single trace of worry. Sometimes they looked at each other, but most of the time they looked down at their food. They seldom smiled, but through the folds of their skin, Jia Jia saw everything that she did not have. She watched them as if they were the last scene of a film, living a happy ending, entirely removed from her own reality. An overwhelming feeling of dejection rose inside her. Head down, eyes closed, she listened to their silence and yearned for it to be hers.

Jia Jia's phone rang loudly in her bag.

'Ms Wu, I have a buyer for you!' Her estate agent sounded like a TV football commentator, all professional enthusiasm. He spent minutes explaining who the potential buyer was: a family of four, an agreeable couple with two children, earning a high income working for American corporations. It seemed as if he was trying to sell the family to her. Finally, after he was satisfied with his expository prologue, he offered Jia Jia the price.

'That's too low. Far too low,' she said.

'The market is bad.'

'Irresponsible!'

'Ms Wu—'

'It has to be higher. A one-bedroom sold for that earlier this year! One-bedroom! Mine's a four-bedroom.'

'I understand—'

'No, you don't seem to. I need more.'

'Ms Wu, it's much more difficult to sell your apartment. I'm already trying my best!'

'You're not trying at all,' she said.

Jia Jia detected her father standing at the entrance of the restaurant speaking to the receptionist. He was looking inside, nodding, and scanning the restaurant for her. The receptionist pointed in Jia Jia's direction, and her father's gaze followed her arm.

'It's much more difficult, you have to understand,' the estate agent continued. 'Because of your husband.'

Jia Jia refocused her attention. 'What?'

'It's not good. Buyers don't like it,' he said.

Her father was walking towards her table now. He looked old. She had not seen him since Chen Hang's funeral, and even then, she had not had much of a chance to study him carefully.

'Your husband killed himself there. It's difficult to ask for a normal price,' the estate agent said.

'He didn't kill himself,' Jia Jia said. 'Tell me, why do you think he would kill himself?'

'Ms Wu, I wouldn't know.'

'He didn't kill himself,' she said again, and hung up.

Her father sat down opposite her and beamed. His eyebrows were grey, long and angled upwards, like dragonfly wings.

'I thought you were in Europe!' he said.

Still maddened by her agent, Jia Jia snapped at her father, 'That was before your son-in-law died.'

The old man sitting next to them looked disapprovingly at her. His wife signalled him with her eyes to mind his own business.

'I see, was it that long ago?' Jia Jia's father laughed. 'When I saw your call, I thought something had happened. Did everything go all right? You said you were moving in with your grandmother.'

'Oh, sure, it was easy.' She handed over the menu. 'It's really good.'

'Yes! You've been here? They make delicious ribs. Vegetables are—'

'The menu. The pages.'

'What?'

'The quality of the paper is good.' Jia Jia pointed at the menu and waited for his reaction. He flipped one of the pages back and forth twice, studied the corner briefly, and lost interest.

'Let me get you some starters,' he said. 'Xiao Fang is stuck in traffic.'

'That woman is coming?'

'Don't say "that woman", it sounds bad. You used to call her Auntie Fang Fang. She just wants to see you.' He summoned the waitress and ordered some pigs' ears, marinated bran dough and cucumber salad.

Jia Jia waited until the waitress had walked away before she spoke quietly, trying to make up for her terrible attitude a moment earlier. 'You look older. Is she taking good care of you?'

'She's found me an acupuncture doctor. My shoulder feels better now.' He patted his left shoulder. 'If you're not feeling well, tell your Auntie Fang Fang, she's done a lot of research on doctors. She's a good woman. Remember when she used to take you fishing?'

He continued talking about Xiao Fang. Jia Jia struggled not to listen. She searched for an appropriate moment, a small opening in his passionate monologue, to ask him about his own family: her family. *What about us?* she wanted to know.

'... after we got married last year,' she heard him say.

His voice sounded distant and hollow, as if it came from the centre of an empty concert hall. Jia Jia squeezed her left wrist with her right hand and realised that she had forgotten to pull up her sleeve to reveal the jade bracelet that she was wearing. It had been a wedding present from her father. That morning, she had checked three times to make sure that she had remembered to put it on, so that when she poured tea for him, he would be able to see it circled around her pale wrist, pine green and translucent. But she had forgotten about it entirely.

She tried to remain composed and courteous, but she must have reacted in some way; her father was looking around uneasily at the waitresses and customers who had turned to look at their table.

'You what?' she asked.

'We got married in December. I'm sorry we didn't tell you, I didn't think it was a good moment.'

Jia Jia searched her mind desperately for something
to say, something that would not blow up this dinner,
that would not drive her father away from her. But she
suddenly could not stop thinking about her mother,
the way she'd lain in the hospital bed, pale and hopeless like a white flower petal that had been tweezed off
its stem.

'Do you have Ma's bronze dragon?' was what she
finally managed to say.

'Dragon?' he asked, still absent-mindedly looking
down at the menu while unfolding his reading glasses.

'Never mind.'

Jia Jia poured a cup of tea for herself and reached
for her chopsticks as the waitress placed the appetisers
between her and her father. She attempted to pick up
a peanut. Her chopsticks kept failing her, though she
had always been skilful at using them. *Beautifully elegant with perfect technique*, a friend of Chen Hang had
once said. What was the matter with her today? The
more she dropped the peanut, the stronger her desire
to pick it up. Finally, she managed to bring it to her
mouth and put it in.

Silence descended. Like a well that had suddenly
gone dry, Jia Jia could think of nothing more to say to
the man sitting in front of her.

'I should leave,' she said and got up from the table.

She rushed past all the square tables, the signs for
the bathroom, the round tables and the reception

desk. Not once did she look back at her father, but she could see him, sitting there alone, and the old couple sitting next to him who were observing what might have been the most curious event of their day.

Someone bumped into her shoulder, apologising. Jia Jia looked up and saw Xiao Fang. She focused on the face of this person whom her father considered to be a 'good woman', trying to read what was on her mind.

'Jia Jia! Are you looking for the bathroom?' Xiao Fang said. This face, too, had aged since they went fishing, years ago.

'Have you, by chance, seen a bronze dragon in my father's home? It's about this big.' Jia Jia held out her hands and indicated that the object was around the size of a big coffee cup. Before Xiao Fang could answer, Jia Jia found she could not look at her face any more. This woman who was here, and her mother who was gone. She lowered her head again and marched down the escalator.

Back at her grandmother's house, Jia Jia crawled under the bedcovers and imagined her father and Xiao Fang sitting at the round table in the corner of the Shanghainese restaurant, devouring a plate of braised pork belly. They were effortlessly in sync, becoming one another, like Leo's parents. They were on the opposite shore of a deep river that Jia Jia could not cross, on an island that had no space for her. Tears came in waves, her throat tight with a strangling pain, and she held her left hand, still wearing the jade bracelet, over her mouth to cover any sounds that she was making.

9

Jia Jia woke with a fear of ageing that left her unable to breathe. She leaned over the basin and stretched the skin of her cheeks with her fingers. Her reflection exposed a few spots that were darkening. She smiled and examined the fine lines at the corners of her eyes and thought for a moment that she saw them stretching away, like grapevines. She stormed out to a nearby mall and spent over one thousand yuan on anti-ageing cream, anti-ageing serum and anti-ageing face mask. She also wanted to buy an eye mask, but finally decided against it.

She returned to the apartment and charged past the living room where her grandmother was feeding the surgeonfish and clownfish in the aquarium. The tank was much taller than the old woman, who stood on a small plastic stool to reach her arm above the rim. Jia Jia thought about helping her. But instead she went into the bathroom, washed her face, spread half a bottle of face mask over her skin like butter, sat on the toilet seat and waited.

For the entire night following her catastrophic meeting with her father, she had kept her phone next to her pillow, the volume turned up, and waited for him to call and take back what he had told her, as if there could have been a chance that he had lied about his new marriage. But he never did. How typical of him not to think of her, Jia Jia thought. The card that Qing had given her, from the gallery, was still untouched on her bedside table, next to the fish-man sketch. None of that – the gallery, selling paintings, her art – seemed important, and she had failed her friend, who must have tried so hard to find her a gallery that was willing to meet her. But Jia Jia felt so tired. Everything she touched seemed to bounce away from her with stronger force.

She washed off the mask after exactly fifteen minutes and went back to her room.

'The biggest mistake people make is keeping it on for too long,' the salesperson had warned her. 'It'll actually extract moisture from your skin.'

She applied the rest of the skin products to her face and felt a little more at ease. Then she directed her attention to her fish-man paintings, taking them out one by one from the cardboard box and studying them. These paintings could hardly be considered art, she decided, and took them downstairs and stuffed them into the rubbish bin outside. There was just one that she wanted to keep. It was, objectively, the worst painting in the box, but there was an honesty and plainness about it that she wanted to preserve. Perhaps it resembled Chen Hang's sketch the most. It did not look like an oil painting – it had no background and no layering, just the body of a fish in the middle of the canvas, painted in greyish strokes that looked like diluted ink. Even the outline of the body was not precisely contoured, as if the fish was somehow emerging and disintegrating at once.

She set the painting on an easel and sat on her bed, trying to visualise its face. She could not go forward any more, not like this. She was going nowhere like this. It was as if she had begun a story with the fish-man long ago, before she could remember, something that had pushed her off her axis, something that demanded an ending now. She had to see the fish-man for herself, to be able to fill out that empty oval on the canvas. For a moment she thought she saw the oval expanding, like a hole that, if left untouched, would ultimately eat up the entire work. The more she stared at it, the more certain she was that she had to finish the painting. But the news of her father's marriage occupied her mind, and she could not concentrate. She had to leave this stifling, yellowing room. She thought about how Chen Hang would take himself away when he needed to. She wondered if she too might go to Tibet.

That afternoon, Jia Jia picked up her phone, scrolled through her contacts list to find Chen Hang's travel agent, and was relieved that she had not deleted her number. The idea of getting away for a few days had given her some energy.

'I want the same itinerary,' she told the woman on the phone. 'I would like to stay as close as possible to the hotels where he stayed, but cheaper ones.'

'I will certainly check and see if we can arrange that,' the woman said. Her tone reminded Jia Jia of the announcer on the subway. Jia Jia held the phone between her ear and shoulder as she scribbled with a sketching pencil into an old beauty magazine.

Day 1:	*Arrive in Lhasa*
Day 2:	*Potala Palace.* ~~*Johang*~~ *Jokhang Monastery (walk around three times)*
Days 3–5:	*Nyingchi*
Days 6–7:	*Guide's home.* <u>*DREAM HERE.*</u>
Day 7 and after:	*TBD. Depends on fish-man.*

'I also want the same guide,' Jia Jia said. 'I don't know his name though.'

'I will check to see if he is available. Would you not like to see Namtso Lake?' the woman said. 'At this time of the year, it should be—'

'No, thank you. That's it for now.'

To accommodate the guide's schedule, Jia Jia's arrangements would not be finalised until two weeks later.

Now that she had a plan, she felt up to going through her unread messages from the night before. Maybe her apartment had been sold at a decent, fair price. Maybe there was somebody who did not know about Chen Hang dying in that bath, or somebody who did not care.

Most of the messages were adverts, but there was indeed a message from her agent, who urged her to ring him immediately. Ms Wan had also sent a text expressing her and her husband's concern for Jia Jia's health.

'Whatever the illness is,' Ms Wan wrote, 'it will all be all right in the end. You have good karma.'

Further down the list, amongst all the junk, she was surprised to see Leo's name. It was a short message.

'Come when you can,' his message said. 'I have a new wine for you.'

Jia Jia called her estate agent first.

'Ms Wu,' he began, without giving Jia Jia a chance to speak. 'You need to understand, I'm trying to do my job but you're not cooperating. I was just being honest with you about your apartment's situation, you see? Ms Wu, I'm just hoping to do the best I can for my clients.'

'Are you finished?' Jia Jia asked coldly. 'I have a beautiful apartment in a beautiful area. And you're telling me that nobody wants to live there? I don't believe you. Call me when you have something new to say.' She hung up.

Jia Jia looked at Leo's text again and checked the time. It was almost noon. Outside the window, willow catkins raided the air, each seed in search of some piece of soil that it could claim as its own.

She and Leo had not spoken since the night of firework skies, in February, when it was still cold. She remembered the fireworks. How beautiful they were. She remembered how she had looked that day, in the orange dress. Immediately she felt nervous. How could she have aged so much in so little time? If she stood naked in front of Leo, would he still want to touch her? She took off her clothes and looked in the mirror. She had lost weight, making the skin on the undersides of her arms look flaccid. She ran her fingers down her neck and tried to focus her attention entirely on what her fingertips were feeling. She wanted her hands to feel in the way that someone else's might. The skin on her shoulders was dry, her breasts were still small, her waist was thinner and her hips were less shapely than she had remembered. She pulled up a chair in front of the mirror and sat with her legs open. She traced her index finger softly from her birthmark to her pubic hair to her clitoris, and found reassurance

in the softness and warmth of what she felt. She
decided that her body was still desirable.

She picked out some evening clothes and waited for
the western sun.

Leo was showing a couple to their table when Jia Jia
pushed open the door. She was wearing a grey dress
with a leather jacket in the same colour. She had lost
weight, Leo thought. He had not known that she was
coming; had not realised how much he had hoped
to see her until he sent that message and began
to wait for a response. Now that she was sitting on
her usual stool in front of him, he seemed to miss
her even more. Her hair hung loose and swayed
against her back when she moved, like a calligraphy
brush.

'I'm sorry I haven't responded to your message,' she
told him.

Leo mixed and served the drinks for his other customers and stopped at the cellar on his way back to
the bar. He took out the bottle of white wine that he
had intended for Jia Jia, a gift from an old friend who
had visited from Tokyo.

'I've saved this wine for you,' he said. 'Japanese wine.
You can't find this in Beijing.'

'That's very kind, really,' she said. 'That you've kept
me in your thoughts. I said terrible things.'

'What are you talking about?'

'To you. I said terrible things to you.'

'I should be the one apologising. But never mind now, I'm glad you've come.' It was true, he was delighted, and he was also truly sorry for what had happened that night.

'I've moved out, to my grandmother's place.' She took a sip of the wine and Leo waited for her reaction. She seemed to have expected it to taste differently but she did not appear displeased.

'What did you do with that horse painting? The one above your sofa,' Leo said.

'I took it with me. It's taking up a lot of space. Will you forgive me for the terrible things I said?'

'Perhaps I should have thought it all through before doing something so rash.'

'I was happy to have met your parents.'

The image of Jia Jia sharing those stories of her mother came to Leo's mind – her dark eyes glowing like pebbles in a clear stream.

'Your mother,' he said. 'Where is she?'

Jia Jia gave the question a moment of thought. Looking away, she answered in a low voice, 'A better place, maybe.'

Then she seemed to remember something and reached into a paper bag that she had brought with her.

'Have you been to Chongqing? My mum bought this from Chongqing, years ago.' She lifted a small lantern out of the bag. 'I thought it would look nice in your bar.'

The oval lantern must have been bright orange when it was new, but the paper had turned a little browner now, lending it a more muted charm.

'I can't take it,' Leo said.

'Oh ... will you not accept it then? I just can't bear to see it hanging in my old room, so lifeless and sad,' she said.

A man caught Leo's attention as he walked up to the counter. He finished his drink and put his empty glass down.

'Ms Wu, good to see you here,' the man said.

His appearance startled Jia Jia.

'I apologise for my tone during our call, Ms Wu, I may have been a bit pessimistic,' the man continued. 'I have managed to find a tenant for you this after-noon. The rent they've offered is not as high as other apartments in your compound, but it's not too bad either. I think you'd be happy.'

'This is my estate agent,' Jia Jia said to Leo.

'Nice to meet you.' The man held out his hand. Leo shook it firmly and told Jia Jia that he would keep the lantern for now, then excused himself from the con-versation. He stepped outside the bar for a moment and looked up at Jia Jia's building across the road. He counted the floors and found her bedroom window. He remembered the last time the light had been on, just over a week ago; he had wondered where she had been.

When he returned, the agent had rejoined his date, leaving Jia Jia observing the lip prints on her wine glass.

'Tell me, since when did we become such strangers?' she said to Leo, still keeping her eyes on the glass.

'We never became strangers. We always were.' He sighed softly – a resolute, solid sigh.

'I see that you're still upset with me,' she said.

He imagined her in a village above the clouds, overlooking the world that he lived in. Her eyes saw everything yet focused on nothing in particular.

'Do you ever feel that sometimes, when something happens to you,' she said, her index finger tapping on the wine glass, 'something deep inside you changes? You can't undo it, and you wonder whether this is the person you want to be. So you just stay, contemplating whether you like your new self until something else happens to you and you start the process all over again. Ever feel that way? If I had met you before I married Chen Hang—'

Leo dropped the dirty glasses he was holding into the sink, making a loud clank and interrupting Jia Jia. 'Don't you think that sometimes we just need to love in the simplest way possible?' he said.

Jia Jia focused her attention fully on him for the first time that night. He saw a sudden influx of emotion in her gaze. Her eyes were black, so black, and Leo thought that he had never seen such wonderful, sorrowful eyes.

'You know what I decided today?' Jia Jia said, her tone determined. 'I'm going to Tibet.'

'You've come to say goodbye,' said Leo. He stopped himself from asking her why she was going to Tibet – she had her own reasons, reasons that had nothing to do with him.

She looked away towards the corner of the room.

'And I am to wait for you?' Leo asked.

'I don't think you should have your life all tangled with mine any longer. I don't *want* you to.' She finished the rest of her wine in one gulp and started filling both of their glasses. While she did that, he just looked at her hands. 'Drink with me tonight.' She clinked her glass against his, on the counter. 'Let's remember this night as a happy one.'

It was a Sunday and the bar was quiet. Jia Jia's agent paid his bill and left, telling Jia Jia that he would send her a lease agreement later on in the week. Leo closed for the evening. He removed his bow tie and stuffed it into his bag without folding it like he usually did.

They drank more and spoke less throughout the night. During the few conversations they did have, Jia Jia laughed in the most honest way Leo had ever seen her laugh. She went behind the bar and started rummaging through his whiskeys; she delved into his bag, pulled out his bow tie, tied it around her own neck and took a picture with his phone. She felt more familiar to him than ever. He became regretful for the life he had never had with her, for the nights they had never spent together behind the lit-up window of their own apartment.

They played disco music from their phones and danced. At some point, Jia Jia made fun of Leo for only owning jazz records. 'How can you dance to these songs?' she said while flipping through his collection.

When the sun peeped through the window, he walked her out the door and told her he loved her.

'How much do you love me?' she answered.

'I couldn't say.'

'Very well.'

She re-tied her hair and headed towards the subway station.

Back in his bar, Leo washed and wiped all the glasses except the one that Jia Jia had used. He sat at the counter for a long while, in the seat at the end, holding her glass. When he finally felt drowsiness creeping over him, he washed the glass thoroughly and hung it above the bar counter with all the others. He arranged Jia Jia's lantern on a small table at the corner of the bar and headed home for a deep, long sleep.

*

When Jia Jia got back to her grandmother's apartment, the aquarium was on fire. There was a single flame the height of a child, thrusting up on one side of the tank from the base towards the ceiling. The corals swayed like metronomes and the fish continued their sluggish, aimless wander, oblivious.

Jia Jia rushed through to the kitchen in search of a container of some sort. Her grandmother was washing rice, and like the fish, she did not have a clue about what was going on. Jia Jia dragged out a bucket from under the sink, knocking over a bottle of cleaning fluid, filled the bucket with water and hauled it back to the living room. She launched it at the tank, spilling half of it on herself. The water seemed to calm the flame somewhat and she began the process again. By this time, her grandmother had emerged from the kitchen and was yelling things.

'Quick, quick, quick,' she kept repeating as she shuffled her feet as fast as she could.

Jia Jia's aunt appeared from her room, saw the flaming tank, and immediately turned to the bathroom to fetch another bucket, all the while shouting at Jia Jia's grandmother to stand out of her way. Jia Jia was not sure how many buckets of water she hurled at the fish tank. She was running out of breath, and her arms refused to lift themselves any more. With one last effort, it was her aunt who managed to put the flame out.

Jia Jia unplugged the aquarium and the blue fluorescent light went off, leaving the fish and coral dull and dusky. The three women stood around the tank, none of them saying anything.

10

Jia Jia's aunt and grandmother began taking turns to sleep at night. They wanted to make sure, they said, that someone would be awake in case the fish tank sparked another fire. An electrician had come during the day and identified the cause of the fire to be an old socket. Ever since then, although the wiring had been replaced, Jia Jia's aunt persisted in pacing back and forth in the living room for hours until her old mother took over the watch at around two in the morning.

Jia Jia needed to finish her work at Ms Wan's home. The restlessness of her aunt and grandmother was oppressive and she needed the balance of the payment for her travels. When Jia Jia phoned to make the arrangements, Ms Wan said that she was in America with her children, and she found it a pity that she could not be there to witness the completion of the painting. The maid will be at home, she told Jia Jia.

In fact, when Jia Jia arrived, it was Ms Wan's husband who was perched on the sofa, blowing smoke rings into the air. She was surprised to find him alone with a bronze ashtray overflowing with Yun Yan cigarette butts, walnut shells and used napkins. From what Jia Jia knew of this man, he was never settled at home during the afternoon. His ponytail was tied lower, but it still revealed the few threads of grey behind his ears. His beard seemed to have grown even longer.

'Sorry for the mess, I didn't know you were coming,' he said. With an ashamed smile, he emptied the ashtray, washed a plate of grapes, and left it on top of the shoe cabinet in the entrance hall for Jia Jia.

'I didn't mean to take such a long break, sir,' Jia Jia said. 'I'm sorry, but I don't think I've ever asked your name.'

'My name is Du Fan, you can call me Old Du. And there's no rush for this painting thing. No rush.' Turning back towards the sofa, Mr Du waved his hand at the painting as if he were brushing someone away.

'Mr Du, if I'm disturbing you today, I can come back when you're not home,' Jia Jia said. 'Say, tomorrow.'

'Not at all,' he muttered under his breath. He searched, with a hint of nervousness, for something to do with his hands. 'I'm going to fetch myself a drink.'

An opened bottle of cognac was already sitting on the dining table and the stench of alcohol filled the suffocating, indoor air. Mr Du poured out a glass.

'Ms Wan and the kids are on holiday in America?' Jia Jia asked as she mixed a palette of blue paint.

'She's in Boston buying duvet covers and pillow-cases,' Mr Du said. 'The kids are going to boarding school there.'

'But the children are so young!' Jia Jia said. 'Do you have a house in Boston?'

'They'll have a guardian there; a good friend of mine. We've known each other since middle school. Wan Lian is coming back in a few days, after they start school. She had originally planned to come back yesterday, you know?'

He held his fist to his ear, pretending he was talking on a phone, and continued, 'But she called me saying, "Oh, the mattress is too soft, their spines will become crooked, I need to buy them a new mattress. I need to buy them shoe cabinets for the new trainers we bought in New York, otherwise the tiny rooms will become smelly. I need to buy a tennis racket for Huihui, I need to buy ballet shoes for Yingying, I need to buy this, I need to buy that." He drank the glass of brandy in one gulp.

'When I was young,' he went on, 'I would've loved to have a soft mattress. The kids need to learn to grow up, and we mustn't spoil them so much, don't you agree? Do you have kids?'

Jia Jia shook her head apologetically, as if to show that she was sorry she could not empathise with him owing to her lack of children.

'Are you married then?' he asked.

Jia Jia thought about it briefly and then shook her head again.

'Hold on.' Mr Du disappeared into the bedroom and re-emerged with an acoustic guitar hung across his body. He pulled out a chair at the dining table, planted himself down, and started tuning his guitar. 'Can you pass me my glass? And my cigarettes.'

Jia Jia delivered his glass and tobacco along with the bronze ashtray that was stained partly black from years of use.

'Let me sing you a song!' He gave his guitar a smack. 'What do you want to listen to?'

'Anything,' Jia Jia said.

'Don't you look down on me, lady. I sang at my jazz lounge every Wednesday night! I'm pretty good. I rarely even sing for my wife. Come on, tell me what you want to listen to!'

'Well then, you pick something.' Jia Jia returned to her painting, picked up her brush, and waited for him to begin.

He lit the last cigarette in the pack and took a drag before balancing it on the rim of the ashtray, making a sort of incense out of it. He picked out a few chords on his guitar, testing the progression to make sure that it was correct. Then he began.

The purity of his penetrating voice surprised Jia Jia; she had expected something raspier. But his singing was like a clear, sunlit day on top of a mountain. It was an English song that sounded familiar to Jia Jia, though she could not identify the title.

His English was well-spoken, but for most of the song he replaced the lyrics with 'la la la' or 'di da la'. The cigarette burned to the end and he ground and crushed it in the ashtray.

'We're getting a divorce,' he said over the final cadence.

Then he strung hard on a dissonant chord, squeezed his eyelids shut, opened his mouth, and cried out loud like a newborn. The skin on his face twisted like a wrung-out towel.

'We had a fight and –' he snapped his fingers – 'just like that, she told me that she wanted to leave me.'

'What about the children?' Jia Jia asked.

He buried his face in his hands and did not answer her question.

'I never thought she'd leave me,' he said finally.

Jia Jia dropped her brush into the cut-out bottom of a plastic bottle. The forest-green paint diffused and tainted the water a milky green colour. She wondered whether Chen Hang would have asked her for a divorce sooner or later and whether he would have married somebody else afterwards. If he had abandoned Jia Jia that way, would she still be painting here today, attending to Mr Du's sobs?

It did not matter any more. Watching Mr Du hold that guitar on his lap, crying as if he was going to let

his heart break in front of her, Jia Jia, strangely, felt a
moment of serenity. As though their hearts had
touched, fleetingly.

'Jia Jia,' Mr Du, raising his head, blurted out suddenly, 'I forgot to ask, are you feeling completely well
now? Was anyone taking care of you while you were
ill?'

'I moved into my grandmother's home,' Jia Jia said.
'My aunt also lives there.'

'Your aunt … Li Chang's wife, right? He's a good
man. Well, let me know if there's anything I can do to
help.' He wiped his tears and smiled.

For the rest of the afternoon, Mr Du sang while Jia
Jia painted. He alternated between English and Chinese
songs, performing everything from jazz to rock bal-
lads to folk music. When Jia Jia knew the song, she
hummed along.

Towards the end of the day, she spent an extra hour
perfecting the beggar's bowl in the centre of the wall
painting. Caressed in the hands of the ancient Buddha,
it gleamed like sapphire.

Mr Du had not spoken much more, and just waved
his hand when Jia Jia said that she had finished. A
horde of men and women were queueing up in front
of the subway by the time she left. She dropped her bag
on the X-ray machine belt at the entrance and a group
of middle-aged women with cameras strapped around
their necks squeezed her through the metal detector.

She let other people board the train first; they seemed in more of a rush to return home. She decided that she would learn how to drive when she returned from Tibet. Jia Jia felt more at ease now that she had finished at Ms Wan's. She did not like to leave things undone, and in some way, it felt like a good omen for her trip. She imagined what Leo would have said if he had seen the wall painting.

He would have praised her for it, she thought.

A few days later, Ms Wan asked Jia Jia to call in. The maid had returned and she was loading bottles into the fridge again. They seemed to be Japanese sake this time.

Mr Du was not home.

'This is exactly what I wanted!' Ms Wan marvelled as she bowed, and traced her index finger over the painting. 'These ponds look like they're real! Oh, and look at the Buddha's eyes! They're so kind ... so caring.'

She knelt down on the marble floor, held her palms together in front of her chest, closed her eyes and prayed as if the Buddha was really sitting in the painting now that it was complete.

'I'll bring you a gift from Tibet,' Jia Jia said.

'Only a kind and pure person like you would be able to complete such a stunning painting.' Ms Wan rose and squeezed Jia Jia's arm. It was a strong clasp that felt ill-matched to her spare, frail body.

'I heard that my husband was home when you came last time,' Ms Wan continued. 'Did he tell you that I'm moving? The air is too bad in the city centre.'

'It's terrible.'

'I don't mind telling you, but we're getting a divorce. The kids are in America now, so I thought it was a good time to get this done. I really can't stay with him any longer. He's never at home. I might as well be living alone. We haven't had a dinner as a family in over two months. Two months! That's more than sixty days. And this time when I came back, the apartment looked like it could have been robbed! It was a mess!' Ms Wan twirled around in a circle and pointed at random things.

Then she picked up her bag and pulled out two piles of new one-hundred-yuan notes bundled together with paper straps.

'How could I spend another day with this man?' she said as she handed the money to Jia Jia. 'Count it again, will you? I'm a little disorganised these days. He's so dirty, you know? Even right after a shower, I still think he's so dirty.'

'He must really love you,' Jia Jia said, unsure of what else she could tell Ms Wan. She stuffed the money directly into the side pocket of her purse, as a gesture of her trust.

'We have two children now,' Ms Wan said. 'Love and passion are not going to get you through a lifetime together. Marriage eventually becomes about two people getting on and living through the days steadily, having a companion when you're old. He doesn't get it.'

'When you move away, what will you do about this painting?' Jia Jia asked.

'I'm sure Old Du will be happy with it. It'll do him good, if you ask me. You have to call me when you're back, all right? I'll have a larger wall in my new living room.' She stretched her arms wide to indicate the immensity of the wall. 'I want another painting. A bigger one!'

Jia Jia agreed and laced up her trainers in preparation to leave.

'Mr Du has a wonderful singing voice,' she said to Ms Wan on her way out.

'Did he sing for you? He used to sing at home from morning to night until we had our second child. It was too loud for me. I prefer a quiet environment.' Ms Wan rubbed her neck and winced. 'I must be getting old. Even on warm days like today, I still always feel like there's wind blowing on my neck.'

She wrapped a blue scarf around herself and escorted Jia Jia out the door.

11

On the day of Jia Jia's flight to Lhasa, she found Xiao Fang waiting for her outside the door. Her father's wife was wearing a rose-coloured silky blouse and blue denim shorts. Her hair was straight and dyed black, held loosely together by a Burberry-chequered clip. Her deep red lipstick made her ageing lips look like dried cranberries, and the shorts were too high and did not suit her. But she had always been like a girl, stubborn and going her own way with a disregard for consequences; she had always, to herself and her family, been the centre of the universe. Now Jia Jia's father had joined that family too.

Jia Jia lifted her suitcase down the front steps. The sky was blue towards the east, but where she was, it had turned grey.

'Jia Jia!' Xiao Fang removed her sunglasses and waved them in the air. 'Are you leaving now? I asked your aunt, she told me you're travelling to Tibet today. I'll drive you to the airport.'

Jia Jia looked around for her father.

'It's just me,' said Xiao Fang. 'Your dad doesn't know that I'm here. He's old now, you know? He has constipation problems and his shoulder hurts all the time. Jia Jia, would you like to move back in with us?'

'Move *back* in?'

'We have two empty rooms, one of them has a bathroom, you can—'

'No,' Jia Jia said. 'I mean, there's no need for that, thank you. I'm living well here.'

Xiao Fang wore a saddened, grim look, like a beaten dog that had just been wronged.

She sighed and said, 'Your aunt is going through tough times too.'

Her voice had the tone of a mother attempting to explain something difficult to her child in the least upsetting way possible. Jia Jia's own mother had never spoken like that: she had simply laughed, cried, loved and hated with all the life in her and never sheltered Jia Jia from any kind of truth – beautiful or shattering. But Jia Jia remembered how, when she was young, she had wished that when her mother stroked her hair at night, she would whisper to Jia Jia that they were going to live as a complete family, that this woman standing in front of her now was only her Auntie Fang Fang and nothing more. Instead her mother had held Jia Jia in her arms, sometimes sobbing into her daughter's hair, and other times rocking her back and forth with a soft, distant smile on her face. She had never attempted to explain anything.

'My old apartment is empty,' Xiao Fang continued. 'If you don't mind, you could stay there. You, your grandmother and your aunt would all be more comfortable.'

'Tell my father to take care. I'll see him when I come back.'

'Think about it, for your aunt's sake. Let me drive you.'

'I've ordered a taxi,' said Jia Jia.

Xiao Fang took the suitcase's handle and helped Jia Jia drag it to the black Toyota that was waiting at the gate of the compound. She beamed and waved her sunglasses again before putting them on. Jia Jia thought of the way her father had lifted the corners of his lips and exposed his teeth at the table in the Shanghainese restaurant.

The airport was swarming with parents and children who were escaping the city for the summer holidays, bumping into each other and charging in all directions, like a herd that was being hunted. Jia Jia had to go through two separate security checks in order to arrive at the check-in counters.

'When on earth are they going to eliminate these pointless checks?' a man's voice shouted somewhere behind her. 'Look at that woman, she didn't put her handbag in! This is utterly useless. And you don't need to pay five people to look after one X-ray machine!'

Jia Jia's phone rang. It was Xiao Fang again.

'Are you all checked in?' she asked. 'What time is your flight?'

'Around seven. I'm queuing up now. What is it?' Jia Jia reached her hand inside her bag and fished out her identification card. The European woman in front of her hurled her backpack onto the belt and left the counter. Jia Jia handed her ID to the airline representative.

'I've just transferred some money to your account. For your trip,' Xiao Fang said.

'I'll send it back once I'm checked in.'

'Just keep it, in case of emergency.'

'I can't keep it,' Jia Jia told her.

'Your father wants you to have it. It's his money. You don't have to feel bad, we both just want to make sure that you have a good time there.'

The clerk attending to Jia Jia handed her a boarding card along with her documents. He circled the boarding time and gate with a red pen and stood to gesture in the direction of the gates. He smiled, sat down and raised his hand for the next customer.

'Jia Jia, let us do something for you,' Xiao Fang continued to say. 'We didn't get to express ourselves in any way when your husband passed on.'

'I don't need the money,' Jia Jia responded.

The queue at security snaked through the entire hall.

'I'll keep it for now and send it back when I return,' Jia Jia yielded so that Xiao Fang would hang up. It worked. Xiao Fang seemed pleased.

Jia Jia was one of the last passengers to board the plane. It was a habit that she had acquired from Chen Hang who despised waiting for others and so always preferred to be the last to scan his ticket. A few minutes after she had squeezed into her seat, a female voice announced the flight number and other details regarding the flight. She then repeated the whole speech in English, and finally left the passengers to talk among themselves in soft murmurs.

Grey clouds floated in the darkening sky. The ten or fifteen minutes during which the plane prepared to take off had always been the most sentimental part of leaving home for Jia Jia. Each time she boarded she would gaze out at the terminal buildings and runways from the sealed cabin, feeling melancholy.

The plane pulled away from the gate, steered towards the runway, and finally lifted off, zooming up and out of Beijing, rising above the clouds and stripping the city away entirely from Jia Jia's vision. After that, there was no sensation that the plane was moving forward any more. It was astonishing, Jia Jia thought, how much human emotions rely on what the eyes can see. When all we can observe is endless condensed water vapour, or the horizon, or the darkness, we feel so incredibly detached from the world below us, as if all ties with our homeland have been cut. And the other passengers, in their designated seats, are just strangers in the cabin going towards the same destination only to separate again.

The hotel was hidden on a small road in the centre of Lhasa city, not too far from Barkhor Street. It was a business hotel and it seemed that nobody had put much thought into its design: a large, concrete shoe-box with a dark red lid for a roof. With a dull, constricting ache in her temples from the high altitude, Jia Jia changed in her room into a long white linen dress. Out on the street, small shops of all kinds sold local produce, electronics, cigarettes. Jia Jia did not have a destination in mind, so she followed two black dogs for a few blocks and arrived at a river that she had seen from her car. One of the dogs had a limping back leg and was drinking from a puddle; the other smaller one had trotted further ahead. It had rained earlier and the bushes on the sides of the street were damp. The river flowed between bare banks, nothing but sand and stone. Jia Jia ripped two pieces of paper from her sketchbook, spread them over the rocks, and sat cross-legged.

She began to draw the fish in the water, though she could not actually see any from where she was. She imagined them matte and grey, like most of the river fish she had seen. They varied in size, but they all charged forward with strong tails, even the fingerling.

She was sketching the fins of a fish when a loud thump came from behind her, and a man cursed. She turned around and saw a scrawny, plain figure lying on his side with a green spiral-bound notebook clutched tight to his chest. A crutch had tumbled in front of him. He wore an oversized caramel shirt with a chest pocket and short sleeves, and washed blue trousers. Jia Jia hesitated before assisting the man back to his feet and handing him his crutch.

'Thank you,' he said, dusting off his clothes. 'Too slippery for a crippled man.'

'You have a Beijing accent,' Jia Jia told him.

He drew his head back in surprise and lifted the crutch slightly in recognition.

'You're from Beijing too? What are you doing here?'

'I was sketching.'

'It's always good to see somebody from Beijing.' He reached out his hand to shake hers. 'What's your name?'

'Wu Jia Jia.'

'You're an artist? I'm a writer. My name is Ren Qi. Show me your sketches!' He moved his head closer to Jia Jia and peered down at her sketchbook. She instinctively took a small step back and he gave her a red-faced look, ashamed for his unintended act of disrespect.

Jia Jia offered him her sketches and he studied each of them intently without making any comment. She realised that he was much younger than she had initially presumed; he must only have been in his twenties.

'Keep drawing! I'm going to sit here and get inspired,' he finally said and slowly lowered himself to the ground. 'Shit! The ground is wet.'

For most of the afternoon, while the sun drew an arc over them, Jia Jia drew fish and Ren Qi focused straight across the river. His eyes were narrowed into slits as if in meditation, and his index finger kept tracing characters on his lap. On occasion, he would tell Jia Jia something about Tibet. Tibet was called the Third Pole of the world. The highest freshwater lake in the world was in Tibet, but the name of it? He could not remember. Almost half of the people on earth depended on the flow of fresh water from the Tibetan plateau. If you did not know the name of a flower here, you should just call it Gesang flower. Every person in Tibet knew how to dance and sing.

'My wife is Tibetan,' he said. 'I can say that indeed, she's a great dancer and singer.'

Jia Jia laughed. 'Are you a tour guide?'

'Wu Jia Jia, I do a lot of research for my writing. Plus, my wife was actually a tour guide. That's how we met. But then she gave up her job and came with me to Beijing.'

He looked across. 'How are the fish?'

This time, like a boy on his first date, he seemed wary of drawing too close.

'Do you like art?' she asked, handing over her sketchbook.

'In theory, yes. I like it a lot, but in theory. Artists these days are trained to be robots. In fact, not just artists, but writers, musicians, too. Even athletes! They paint or write or play the same thing over and over again. The same birds and mountains, the same characters and stories. But fundamentally, Wu Jia Jia, we're still human, of course, so the occasional deviations away from the mechanical become either absolutely brilliant or utterly disastrous. And we all live for those bursting moments of brilliance.'

He leafed through the book, fetched a cigarette out from behind his ear and started smelling it.

'Well, looks like I'm mechanically drawing fish,' Jia Jia said.

'You know what? I think there's something here. Something meaningful.' He held one of the pages in his hand and flipped it back and forth. Then he ripped it out.

Jia Jia snatched the sketchbook away from him.

'This one is the best. Keep it in your wallet,' he said. 'You can throw away the rest. But this one has emotion. It's as if ...' He held the paper against the sun and thought for a moment. 'It's as if its little belly contains all the pride and loneliness in this world. It reminds me of my wife.'

'Prideful and lonely. Is that what your wife is like?'

He handed the paper to Jia Jia.

'We're all like that, most of the time. The lonely part, at least,' he said.

Jia Jia studied her sketch. All these years of drawing and painting: it was as if she had been playing squash, bouncing balls off a wall in an isolated room. Nobody had ever told her that her art had emotion – most of the time, her professors had said the opposite – and she was not quite sure what Ren Qi meant.

'My wife disappeared a month ago,' Ren Qi said. 'She just went out to the hair salon one morning and never came back. The police couldn't find her either. I couldn't bear waiting at home every day, so I came here to look for her. I was thinking that maybe she'd come back to her birthplace.'

'Was she born here, in Lhasa?'

'No, no. She was born in this village here.' He took out a folded map from his notebook and pointed at a spot towards the south-eastern part of the region,

along the route that connected Tibet to Sichuan. 'I'm
going to go there in a few days, after I've met some of
her friends here in Lhasa.'

The village was a small dot on a map, one among a
constellation of identical dots representing the countless villages that aligned the road. Jia Jia, at that
moment, envied Ren Qi his clear destination. He kept
the map open a little longer and then slipped it back
into his notebook. He did not ask Jia Jia where she was
heading.

They parted before nightfall.

'Good to have met you, artist Wu Jia Jia.' Ren Qi
held out his hand and Jia Jia shook it firmly. His palm
was rough like ginger.

Jia Jia watched the outline of his figure as he hob-
bled over to a stone bridge and started to cross the
river. She called out to him.

'Can you help me?' she shouted. 'I'm looking for a
fish-man!'

He hopped on his good leg and turned around.

'Sure! Where do we find him?' he yelled back over
the sound of the water.

'I don't know!'

He held his notebook behind his ear, indicating that
he could not hear her.

'I said I don't know! My husband knew, but he's
dead!'

'Oh, fuck!'

Jia Jia picked up the bottom of her white linen dress and ran to the bridge. He waited in the middle, and she made her way towards him.

'Give me your phone,' she said, catching her breath. He took it out of his pocket and she typed her number in and saved it. 'Here. Call me when you've found your wife, and then come and help me. I'll be looking for the fish-man.'

That night, it rained again and the air smelt like clay. Jia Jia swallowed a few painkillers for her headache and waited for them to take effect. Every time she felt herself falling asleep, her own heartbeat would wake her, as if there was a little person trapped in her heart, pounding on the walls. Finally, unable to breathe in the room, she went out for a walk, dressed in her emerald silk robe. She found a corner in the hotel's courtyard where a few thin, straight trees grew next to one another. She sat down on the rock beneath them. The rain trickled through the black umbrella of leaves and landed on her in cold, heavy droplets; a bit of rain would clear her head, she thought. The dog from the morning with the broken leg trotted past Jia Jia and looked back at her. Shivering from the cold, she smiled at the animal. It approached her, as if it pitied her. It was a skinny creature and reminded her of Ren Qi. She noticed that it was quivering, too.

'Let's go,' she said.

She stood and the dog followed her to the bottom
of the staircase where it spun in a few circles before
lying down.

Back in her room, Jia Jia undressed and climbed
into bed. The rain drummed against the windows
until morning. And she lay half-awake, her heart
pounding strong and fast, tapping to the rhythms of
water.

12

The Tibetan guide never stopped talking. He called himself T.S., short for something that Jia Jia had already forgotten. T.S. remembered her husband, he told her, because he never forgot a Beijing customer. He had lived in Beijing for a year and learned what he called some 'authentic Mandarin' there, even had a local girlfriend. But of course he did not want to stay in Beijing, he told her, he was proud of his home and wanted to return to promote his culture. He had aspired to become a tour guide and his ambitions had come true. Chen Hang had been his twentieth Beijing customer, and Jia Jia was his thirty-second.

Chen Hang's trip had gone mostly according to plan, T.S. recalled, until one morning when he had asked to cancel his final destination.

'We were supposed to go to the Lamaling Monastery,' T.S. said, scratching his head. 'But your husband was a little weird that morning. He seemed to be very angry when I met him at the hotel, and he yelled at me, yes, he really did, he yelled at me, "Forget all these temples, I've seen enough temples, let's go somewhere else."'

The two men had sat down in the hotel lobby with a map of Tibet, and T.S. had suggested every sight within a day's drive that he thought could possibly have interested Chen Hang. Chen Hang had listened and nodded intently without saying a word, and finally he had decided, 'Let's go to your village.' T.S. had explained that his home village was far too underdeveloped, and without proper tourist accommodation or restaurants: where was Chen Hang supposed to sleep and eat? T.S. had suggested that perhaps Chen Hang could stay in a larger city nearby, and if he wanted to visit T.S.'s home, they could make a day trip.

'I'll sleep in your house,' Chen Hang had responded. 'I come from a humble background too. I can sleep anywhere.'

'He stayed in the room that used to belong to me and my brothers. They both moved out after they got married.' T.S. made a thumbs-up gesture and said, 'Your husband was not boasting, he really didn't seem to mind the poor life in the countryside. He even helped out in the qingke fields!'

Jia Jia understood then that her careful itinerary might be in vain. She considered going directly to T.S.'s village, but she decided to visit all the temples anyway and pay particular attention to every detail, trying to extract for herself some meaning from it all. Over the next few days, when she came across paintings or objects involving fish, she stood in front of them and prayed. But the fish-man left no clues for her.

It was not until the drive towards Nyingchi, while she was snoozing on the back seat of the car, that the fish-man appeared in her dream. She seemed in the dream to have no memory of anything that had happened to bring her there: Chen Hang's dream, his death, the sketch, Leo, moving out, the wall painting, her trip, Ren Qi. She was alone with the fish-man in a boundless white room and the fish-man was swimming in the air away from her. Jia Jia's legs were weak and trembling, and she was sitting on the ground without casting a shadow in any direction. Puzzled, she called out to the fish-man, not because she recognised it as the one thing she had been looking for, but because it was the only creature in sight.

The fish-man must have heard her. She was loud enough.

'Don't wait for me for dinner,' it repeated in a rusty voice. 'Don't wait for me. Go ahead and start. Where the hell am I anyway?'

It waved its fin in the air as it spoke, swimming forward without acknowledging Jia Jia's cry for help. Jia Jia crawled towards it with her elbows on the

ground, dragging her legs behind like a wounded sol-
dier. She swore at the fish-man.

'You bastard! Help me, you cold-blooded shit! Fine!
Leave me!' she yelled.

When she woke up, she found they had arrived at
the hotel where she was supposed to spend the next
two nights, and she could not remember how the
dream had ended. She locked the door of her room
that afternoon; she wanted to make a rough pencil
sketch while the image was fresh in her memory, so
that when she returned to Beijing she could try to
paint the fish-man again. She made sure to be as
meticulous as possible with the body, and found that
the more the fish-man took shape, the more she began
to feel a balloon of hope expanding within her. With
every line her pencil drew, her heart pounded faster
and her muscles tensed. When she had completed the
body, hands shaking from having clutched the pencil
too tightly, she held it next to the one she had found
by the bath at home.

Nothing looked alike. With the two drawings in
front of her, her feeling of hope, as if having under-
gone a chemical reaction, transformed into fury inside
her. She felt as though she had reached the sudden
end of a long, arduous road. What was she doing,
making pictures like a child, betting her hopes of con-
clusions on meaningless drawings? Did she even know
how to do anything else?

Jia Jia phoned the hotel reception and asked for a pair of scissors. While she waited, she took nail clippers from her bag and began cutting and tearing up her drawings of fish. She started with her sketchbook, ripping out those fish she had drawn on the day at the river, the 'mechanically drawn' pictures, as Ren Qi had observed. She wanted to slice through all of them at the same time, but the pile was too thick, so she shredded them one by one and flushed them down the toilet. Then she took out the paper that was folded inside the zipped compartment of her wallet.

'This one has emotion,' Ren Qi had said.

A young woman in a long black skirt delivered the scissors. Standing at the open door, Jia Jia cut the drawing in two, in front of the woman, right down the middle. There it went, the drawing that had emotion. As the part with the fish head fell to the ground, a look of panic and unease rose to the woman's face. She stood stunned, her mouth slightly open.

'Can I help you?' Jia Jia asked, wanting to sound calm but her voice getting caught, as though there was something stuck in her throat that she could not swallow. She pulled her sleeves down over her hands, dug the nails of her left hand into her right palm, cleared her throat, and opened her mouth again.

The young woman spoke first. 'So sorry, so sorry, sorry,' she interrupted Jia Jia and darted off, her skirt getting trapped between her legs as she scuffled quickly around the corner.

Jia Jia stepped into the hallway and lingered for a moment, waiting for something to happen. Nobody came. Back at her desk, she gazed at the two fish-man drawings, the one she had just finished and the original sketch from Chen Hang. These were the only two that she had not destroyed. Finally, she held them one on top of each other, and cut them both down the centre.

Somebody tapped on her open door. She heard T.S.'s voice.

'Ms Wu, are you ready to go to dinner?'

Jia Jia stood up. Perhaps going out to dinner would do her good right now. She went into the bathroom to tie her hair. When she came out, T.S. was standing at the desk, pointing at her sketch.

'I've seen this guy,' he said.

He picked up the two parts of her drawing and pieced them together.

'Actually,' he continued, 'it's not exactly the same. But we have a sculpture like this in our village, a fish's body with a human's head. It's been there a long time, ever since I was a child, carved from a big log next to the stream in the forest. According to the stories, an old man we call Grandpa once saw the shape of a fish in the log, and decided to make it into a sculpture. How do you know about it?'

'Did Chen Hang see it as well?' Jia Jia asked.

Her earlier dread vanished as though it had never existed. The dead end was an illusion; she had found another road. This sculpture, whatever it was, must have had something to do with Chen Hang's dream. He must have seen it.

'Let's go. Let's leave now. Meet me at the car in ten minutes,' she said. 'Let's go to your village.'

'I think it's too late today. It's already getting dark, it'll be better to stick to—'

'What do you know about the fish-man?'

'What fish-man?'

'The one you were just talking about! The fish-man on the log in your village!'

'Fish-man? Oh, fish-man!' He threw his head back and laughed. 'That's a great name! I should tell Grandpa about it. We've always referred to it as "the sculpture". The "fish-man" sounds so much more mythical. I'm going to come up with stories about the fish-man to tell the kids in the village. They'll love it.'

Jia Jia walked up to him and gripped both of his shoulders in her hands, shaking him hard. He must have understood how determined and desperate she was, because he went quiet, slackened his posture, and caved his chest in to make himself smaller. Then he rushed out of her room to prepare the car, without saying a single word more.

*

The moon glowed behind a thin veil of clouds, and the night was wet with a fresh breeze blowing. They were high in the snowy mountains. As T.S.'s Jeep curved around the bumpy road, Jia Jia saw a handful of villagers drinking and dancing next to a bonfire, its flames lighting up prayer flags attached to poles in the ground, and hanging from the tops of houses.

An old man with braided grey hair, dressed in a tan robe, made his way slowly towards the vehicle. T.S. parked it and called out to him in Tibetan. The old man gestured back and T.S. yelled towards a two-storey farmhouse, built from white bricks, not far from where he had parked.

'That's the old man we call Grandpa – he can't speak,' the guide explained. 'He's like a real grandfather to me. I think he came to our village when my mother was young.'

Momentarily, Jia Jia was able to see the old man's face clearly in the light from the fire. There was something that felt familiar in his stare, which penetrated through her as if she were glass. It was as though he was a long-time neighbour with whom she had never spoken, someone who knew everything about her yet kept it all a secret. She caught his eye and looked away.

A stocky, middle-aged woman came out, with a surprised expression, and guided the old man back towards the house. As she walked, she kept turning to look at Jia Jia.

'That woman is my mother,' T.S. explained as he pulled Jia Jia's suitcase towards the farmhouse. 'Nobody really knows where Grandpa came from. My mother told me that he just turned up one day, but she doesn't remember when exactly. She was still a child. Our village used to be much more isolated. Now, since the highways have been built, we get many more cars passing by. My mother thinks that Grandpa came during the time when they first started to build roads connecting to the larger villages. Maybe he came from another village nearby.'

The family managed to spare a room for Jia Jia. T.S.'s mother offered her some stir-fried cabbage and scrambled eggs, apologising for the fact that she only had a little food left from dinner. The walls in the house were a teal colour, and on the section of wall next to the shrine for Buddha statues, there was a painting of yellow Tibetan horns. Almost all the furniture was made out of wood the colour of raisins – the sofa, the tables, the shrine. The entire house smelt like goat's butter mixed with incense – a pungent smell that had been soaked up over the years by the bricks and the wood.

Jia Jia had immediately wanted T.S. to show her to the river bed to see the log, but it was late and she felt reluctant to disturb what seemed like a long-awaited family reunion. Anxious for the next day, she slid open the window to let in the cool, moist air. The bonfire was dimming and only four men remained, drinking qingke wine. They each held a cowboy hat in their lap. Jia Jia sat down on an embroidered cushion and tried to decipher what the family was talking about next door. Grandpa seemed to live with them; for Jia Jia this was strange, as her family would never have taken in an unrelated elderly guest. She dug out a cigarette from her bag, rested it between her lips for a moment, and then struck a match and lit it.

Ren Qi had not phoned her. Jia Jia trusted that he would keep to his promise, because he seemed like an honest man. Perhaps he had not found his wife yet? Might he have told her this, at least?

While she recalled her conversation with him, she rubbed through her skirt at the kite-shaped birthmark on her thigh. She still found herself fidgeting with it like this, as if she could erase it. Her headache came pounding back harder than before and she gently brought her legs towards her chest and hugged them. She watched the men leave the bonfire, and the fire die out, until the throbbing pain faded and numbed. Hearing the laughs and chatter floating in from the living room, she covered her legs with a blanket woven by T.S.'s mother and leaned against the wall, until the half-moon faded into daylight.

13

The fish-man was not big. Jia Jia could easily have missed it, had she gone searching for it herself. It was part of a tree trunk about knee-high, balanced on a large rock next to a stream. The fish-man was carved onto the surface of the wood, apparently without much care; it was not really a sculpture at all. It was barely a fish or a man, and without T.S. pointing it out to her, she would probably have failed to recognise it. Someone had tied a red string around its neck and fastened it into a bow.

'It's been here for a long time, for as long as my memory goes back,' T.S. told her. 'Grandpa comes down once in a while to make sure it's still here. What do you think is so special about it? Grandpa would never tell me.'

'Did my husband come here?'

'Not that I know, but he could have.'

Jia Jia squatted down in front of the log and ran her fingers over the eyes of the fish-man, which were made from oval holes with stones wedged into them. The log had no branches and no trace of having had any cut off. The deep wood grain made the creature look as though it had wrinkles all over its face and body, so that it appeared much older than she had imagined. Jia Jia tried to move the log but it remained stubbornly fixed to the rock beneath. On its blank side a large number '1' was carved out.

Jia Jia stood up. She needed to clear her head. On their way back to the village, T.S. suggested that she should help out in the qingke fields in order to, as he put it, 'experience farming at least once in your life'. And so for the rest of that day she did, more than anything to keep herself grounded, to feel the soil on her hands and the earth beneath her feet.

Yaks roamed everywhere in the village, feeding on grass or whatever was left in rubbish bags on the streets. Jia Jia wrapped a scarf over her head to shade herself from the sun while T.S. taught her how to weed. She had never even gardened before.

'Always make sure to take out the roots,' he told her over and over again. When he had made sure that she knew what qingke sprouts looked like, he left her alone to work on a small patch of field.

She worked slowly and tried to do exactly what T.S. had shown her, her exposed arms burning from the sun. Occasionally, when she stood up straight to stretch her back, Jia Jia looked towards the curve on the road. When she and T.S. had arrived the day before, Grandpa must have been sitting at home and spotted them coming. Should she ask him about the carving? Knowing that Grandpa did not like to talk, would it be impolite to enquire too much?

At nightfall, Jia Jia had dinner with T.S.'s family. Grandpa, as the eldest, sat at the table first, followed by T.S.'s mother, and lastly, T.S. and Jia Jia. T.S.'s mother had fried some potatoes and stir-fried some vegetables. She taught Jia Jia how to eat tsampa. She had already mixed the barley flour with some buttermilk tea, and Jia Jia was told to squeeze the dough into balls with her palm.

'You have to wash it down with some buttermilk tea,' T.S.'s mother said, in her strong accent. 'It can be difficult to swallow without some liquid.'

Jia Jia did not eat much; the flavours were too pungent. While she ate, she observed Grandpa. He did not smile, only chewed his food and sipped loudly on the tea that T.S.'s mother kept pouring for him.

'You're not used to Tibetan food,' T.S.'s mother said to Jia Jia, smiling.

'It's my first time here,' Jia Jia explained.

'My son told me your husband is Chen Hang. I remember him. He quite enjoyed Tibetan food.'

'Yes. I can imagine.' Jia Jia paused and picked up her cup of tea and rested it in her palms, hoping that T.S.'s mother would not ask more about her husband.

'I have something I want to ask Grandpa,' she said. 'I know he doesn't speak much. But I'd still like to ask.'

T.S.'s mother looked at her son and then at Grandpa. The old man nodded and reached his hand into the bowl of dough.

'The fish-man on the log. I want to know more about it,' Jia Jia said, her eyes on Grandpa. Grandpa looked at the ball of dough in his hand for a while and Jia Jia could not tell whether he was going to respond.

'He doesn't speak about that log.' T.S.'s mother finally broke the silence.

'He doesn't speak about anything, really,' T.S. added. 'I'd give up if I were you.'

Looking between T.S.'s mother and Grandpa, Jia Jia could tell there was something that both of them knew, but neither of them wanted to say. Grandpa drank his tea and would not even look at Jia Jia, though she kept her gaze on him. T.S. turned to her with a 'told you so' expression, and Jia Jia knew she could not ask more, at least not tonight.

After dinner, the village eased into slumber. Windows dimmed one by one, until all Jia Jia could see was the moon and the constellations. She could not sleep, her mind was restless and the skin on her arms was stinging from sunburn. She put on a jacket, grabbed her phone to use as a torch, and crept out of the farmhouse. The path towards the stream was easy to remember – up the hill, past the fields, and a five-minute trek in the direction of the pig-shaped mountain. She could hear animals but was unable to identify what they were, and she thought about turning back.

With everything that had been happening, Jia Jia would not have been surprised had she found that the log had moved by itself. She wrapped her arms around it and tried again to pick it up but it was heavy. Instead, she gently touched her forehead to it, feeling the damp, chilled wood against her skin. Alone with it now, it was as if she had known the fish-man for a long time. She listened to the sounds of the stream, her skin against the log, waiting for something. A sign, perhaps. But everything around her was moving – the water, the trees, the insects – except for the log. The log remained still and silent. She lost track of how long she stayed with it.

Eventually she made her way back, and saw the outline of a man hobbling on the muddy road. She felt a sudden panic: she should have brought a kitchen knife with her, at least. The man was turning towards her: he must have heard her approaching. She shone her torch at him, hoping that it was just T.S. out looking for her.

But it was not him. The man had a crutch under his arm.

'Ren Qi?' she whispered loudly.

He held his arm over his eyes and shouted, 'Can you turn off the damn light?'

She hurried towards him and switched off her torch. 'It's me!'

It took a moment for him to recognise her, and when he did, he shouted again, 'Wu Jia Jia!'

She quickly covered his mouth with her hand. 'Shhh,' she whispered. 'Do you want to wake the entire village? How did you find me? I've been waiting for you to call.'

'I was looking for my wife. I didn't expect to find you instead!' He laughed and smacked her on the back.

'Looking for your wife out here in the middle of the night?' She laughed too and tugged on his arm. 'Come. Let me show you something.'

'Oh! You found him?'

'Quiet! You're being loud again.'

Ren Qi trailed behind Jia Jia, forgetting to whisper and cursing when he tripped.

He pointed to a plant and said, 'That looks like cannabis!'

'I'll wait for you if you want to pick it,' Jia Jia said, smiling.

When she presented the wooden log to Ren Qi, she could not see his reaction but imagined it to be one of ridicule for her obsession. He stood there, his back to her, quiet as stone, and looked at the thing for a while. But when she moved around to join him, she found that she had been wrong. There was no ridicule, no intrigue, in fact there was nothing in his expression. He was looking at the fish-man but not paying attention to it, as if he were walking on a busy road of pedestrians and the fish-man were merely another one of many faces. She had expected too much, for a stranger to take an interest in a silly wooden log.

'My husband's name was Chen Hang.' Jia Jia spoke softly. 'It was an unexpected kind of death. Weird, really. Upside down in the bath in our apartment.'

She let out a little snigger and despised herself for it. She climbed onto the rock and crouched down, showing Ren Qi Chen Hang's position when she had found him in the bath. Realising how absurd she must look, she quickly straightened her back and held out a hand to help Ren Qi up. They sat with the log in between them.

'He drew a picture before he died,' she said. 'A creature from a dream he'd had here, in this village. A fish-man. It has the face of a man with a big forehead. So big that when you're looking at it, it's difficult to focus your attention on his other features. But my husband sketched the whole face out, even the wrinkles on its lips. From the neck down, it's a fish. But that part is less detailed.'

'Fish body, man head,' Ren Qi said, writing characters on the surface of the rock with his index finger. 'And with a big forehead.'

'I wasn't there when he drew it.' She paused. 'When I remember Chen Hang, I see him holding a hotel-room pencil, sketching the fish-man. I wasn't even there for that, but that's what I remember. Strange, isn't it?'

'I have to say that is very strange.' He took out a cigarette.

'Give me one,' Jia Jia said and looked in the pack, selecting the one that she most wanted to smoke. She lit it first, and then held the flame up for his. He hesitated to begin with, but eventually took a deep breath, shook his head, and turned towards the flame.

'I've been trying to reconstruct his sketch with both oil and pencil,' Jia Jia continued. 'But every fish-man I've attempted so far has been faceless. I can't recreate its face.'

Ren Qi sighed and they listened to the stream together until Jia Jia spoke again.

'What did you mean, that you were looking for your wife here?' she asked.

He took his cigarette from his mouth and said, 'This is her home. I hoped that she'd have come back.'

Jia Jia remembered the dot he had shown her on his map, back in Lhasa. He had not told her the name of the village, but somehow it did not surprise her that it should be this one. It felt right for him to be here, for them to be here together, both searching for something.

'Tomorrow let's ask the family I'm staying with. If your wife is from here, they should know her,' Jia Jia said.

'I have a feeling, though. A feeling from my gut, you might say, that she's not here right now. I can't say why, this place just feels so foreign.' Ren Qi touched the log. 'So cold, even.'

'Let's see in the morning,' Jia Jia smiled. But Ren Qi was looking straight ahead.

'You know, you're a good artist,' he said. 'You're good, and I mean it. I've seen you draw. So what can possibly get in the way of you painting a guy's face? Think about it. Maybe it's just not meant to be yours to paint.'

Jia Jia flicked the lighter on and stared into the flame. 'I've always been fascinated by things related to water but I've also been a disaster at painting any of them. Maybe I'm just setting myself up to fail.'

'Wrong.' Ren Qi seized the lighter and turned Jia Jia by her shoulders to face him. 'You have to come up with a new face to put down on your painting,' he said, pointing a finger at Jia Jia's nose and then at an arbitrary spot on the rock. 'Not the one your husband drew.'

They were quiet again for a long while, Jia Jia floating in thought, feeling the remnants of his touch at her shoulders.

'What are you always writing with your finger?' Jia Jia asked.

'Oh, I barely even realise I do it, probably just as you don't know you always do *this* with that lighter you're always holding.' He clenched his left hand into a thumbs-up fist and tapped his thumb on his fingers a few times.

'I do that a lot?'

'Yeah. Quite a bit.' He laughed. 'Even when you don't have a lighter. You want a drink?' He pulled out a bottle of qingke wine from his backpack.

They took turns drinking from the bottle. The alcohol burned a little as it entered Jia Jia's stomach, making her feel alive.

'I imagine this to be the drink of the heavens,' Ren Qi said. 'There's a purity to it. Don't you think?'

Jia Jia laughed.

'I'm serious,' Ren Qi said.

'It tastes more like the drink from hell to me. Sour and rotten.'

'But you do agree that it tastes like it's from another realm.'

Back at the edge of the village, Grandpa was pacing around an empty plot of land with a long stick in his hands. As Jia Jia and Ren Qi approached him, they saw that he was digging holes in the ground and planting something into them.

'It's almost two in the morning – what could he possibly be planting?' Jia Jia whispered.

'He's old. He can't sleep.'

Ren Qi was unable to whisper. Grandpa turned around and waved at them, motioning for them to join him. Unable to refuse, Jia Jia made her way over, a little dazed, careful not to step on whatever it was that Grandpa had just planted. Ren Qi followed, dragging his bad leg behind the good one. The old man handed Jia Jia his stick and beckoned to her to replicate his movements. She felt compelled to obey and started digging until she had a hole that was about a hand's span deep in the soil. Grandpa shook his head, suggesting that the hole was too shallow. And so Jia Jia continued, while Ren Qi cheered her on, until Grandpa told her to stop by pulling her hand away. He fetched something from his pocket, signalling for her to bury it in the hole.

It was a flower bulb. After Jia Jia had planted it and covered it with soil, Grandpa suggested Ren Qi plant one as well.

'No, no. I'm not the gardening kind of man,' Ren Qi explained, yawning, as if Grandpa's authoritative aura had no effect on him. Grandpa gave a small frown and proceeded to dig the next hole.

Ren Qi had not managed to find accommodation yet, so Jia Jia offered to let him sleep in her room. She asked Grandpa for permission, and he nodded in approval. Ren Qi took a blanket from his backpack, spread it over three cushions, and nestled against the far wall.

'The worst days give us the best memories,' he muttered. 'My wife told me.'

His breathing deepened and steadied while Jia Jia lay still on her side and rested her finger gently on her birthmark.

She woke again in deep, dark, cold waters. She knew this well by now; this real, biting chill. Instinctively, she searched for the silver fish that shimmered like the North Star, kicking her legs and propelling her body upwards. Something appeared in the distance; the fish had grown to be much bigger than before. She changed direction and trailed the creature, treading harder, fighting off the bitter cold, and each aching breath felt as though it was going to be her last.

The way this creature swam was different – it swayed its tail more. It reminded her of the fish-man in her dreams. She was holding hands with someone. The hand was warm and felt as though it belonged to Chen Hang, plump and strong.

'Keep going, Chen Hang,' she thought she said, and kept her eyes fixed on the creature for fear that if she looked away it would vanish again. She was not going to let it disappear from her sight this time, not this time.

But it did. It was gone. And holding her hand, kneeling next to her on the wooden floor of the farmhouse with the moonlight on his face, was Ren Qi, with his cold palms dry like ginger.

14

'Look outside,' said Ren Qi. He gave Jia Jia's hand a firm squeeze and then let go of her.

Jia Jia looked. Though it was still dark, she could see the outlines of at least a dozen people gathered beneath the house.

'Put on a jacket – let's go down.'

Ren Qi took his crutch, opened the door, and clambered down the narrow staircase.

Jia Jia felt the solidity of the floor beneath her, the weight of the Tibetan plateau air, the vivacity of her cells, the flowing blood in her veins. The water, had it gone? The creature was lost with it as well. Did Ren Qi see it all? And now something was happening outside, in a landscape where there was air and soil, and where water had its boundaries.

Whatever was going on, it must be important. Even the neighbours had been woken up. Could it be that Ren Qi's wife had returned? He was so quick to join the get-together. It would be delightful news, something to rejoice in. But Jia Jia's body ached all over as if her tendons were rupturing. She could not imagine herself shaking the wife's hand, congratulating the couple on their reunion. She lay back down and rested her arm on her forehead, waiting for the night to retreat into calm.

But people began climbing the stairs and clomping around. Ren Qi thrust his crutch at the door and burst back in.

'You fell asleep again?' His hoarse voice erupted into the room.

'What is it?' Jia Jia asked.

Without moving, she waited for him to announce the return of his beloved; the ripe fruit of his laborious hunt. She waited for him to tell her that he regretted not being able to accompany her any more on her quest, that he wished her the best of luck for her future endeavours, and that he, unquestionably, would learn from his past and live a life of gratitude from now onwards.

But instead, he said, 'The old man is gone.'

Jia Jia turned her head to face him.

'Get up.' Ren Qi fumbled through Jia Jia's bag and tossed her a jacket. 'Hurry.'

Jia Jia did not know what he meant, whether he was speaking about Grandpa or somebody else, and whether he meant that a man had gone missing or had died some time during the night. What lifted her from the floor was the fact that Ren Qi's wife had, for the time being, chosen to remain missing. Only a few minutes earlier she thought she had been left behind.

Ren Qi, waiting for her at the doorway, impatiently inclined his head towards the room where Grandpa usually slept with the children. The others were nearby, discussing something noisily in Tibetan.

Jia Jia joined him and the two of them walked past the family room and kitchen to the hallway on the other side. T.S. spotted them first.

'Were we being too loud?' T.S. asked, and gave Ren Qi a confused look.

'This is my friend, Ren Qi,' Jia Jia explained. 'He arrived late last night and Grandpa told us that he could stay in my room.'

'You saw Grandpa? He's gone missing.' T.S.'s nose was red and his eyes were moist.

'We saw him outside, two or three hours ago. He hasn't come back?' Jia Jia asked.

'It's strange,' T.S. said. 'My mother woke up and she couldn't hear a thing. That's not normal, she thought – usually there are the dogs or the wind or the men snoring. It's never so quiet. So she checked the house and that was when she found that Grandpa's bed was empty. The kids were all there, asleep. But Grandpa was gone and nobody heard him leave. We've searched everywhere in the village.'

T.S. put his hands on his waist and turned his head to look around the family room, as if Grandpa might suddenly appear again in a cloud of smoke. Ren Qi had left them briefly and was now returning with something clasped in his hand.

'Look at this,' he said to Jia Jia.

He held out his palm and revealed a miniature wooden figure of the fish-man. It was about the size of a teacup. On the back, the number '9' was carved.

'There's an entire shelf of them,' he added.

Jia Jia navigated past the family and into the bedroom, Ren Qi limping behind. Indeed, there was a collection on the windowsill next to Grandpa's bed, some carved from wood, others from stone. The faint gleam from a single light bulb cast the figures the colour of persimmon. In the shadows next to the collection was a stack of photos. The one on the top showed a little boy posing in a Mickey Mouse sweatshirt next to a donkey. It was taken at the entrance to the village.

'Looks like me when I was young,' Ren Qi commented. 'Just a bit chubbier.'

Jia Jia picked up the pile and began studying the photos.

'Grandpa took these,' T.S.'s mother said as she walked up behind Jia Jia. 'He saved a traveller from a wolf once, and to thank him, the traveller gave him a camera. Ever since then, Grandpa's photographed all kinds of people who visited this village. The camera is his little treasure. And he didn't even take it with him.'

T.S.'s brother entered the room, out of breath, and said something in Tibetan.

'He couldn't find Grandpa in the mountains,' T.S.'s mother translated, shaking her head. 'We'll call the police. I can only hope that the wolves haven't taken him.' Her voice trembled a little.

The photos came in all sizes and many had all kinds of stains on them. Jia Jia could tell that a handful of them had been taken decades ago, when the village was poorer, and so were the travellers. In the newer ones, most stood with their cars, while some of the more daring seemed to have been high-altitude mountain-biking. Jia Jia flipped through the endless enthusiastic smiles, passionate hugs and exhausted thumbs-up of the tourists, until the most ordinary photo took its turn at the top of the pile. In the frame was half of an army-green three-wheeled motorbike, piles of wet mud on a road, a blurry black dog, and a couple walking away from the camera. On the bottom-right corner was the date stamped in red: *19 06 87*.

Unlike the other photos, in which the subjects were all posing for the camera, this one looked like a mistake: a moment not extraordinary enough to be captured. Perhaps it was for that reason that Jia Jia felt attracted to it over the others. The woman was wearing a red cardigan and the man held a beige jacket in one of his hands; his other hand was holding the woman's elbow to make sure that she would not fall.

'I remember this couple.' T.S.'s mother squinted her eyes at the photo. 'The woman was pregnant. I remember that they were from Beijing too, or was it Tianjin? It was somewhere up north. They stayed for quite a long time, and became good friends with Grandpa.'

T.S.'s mother gently lowered herself to the bed and told Jia Jia and Ren Qi to sit next to her. Since she had woken up in the middle of the night, she was not in her Tibetan robe and her hair had not yet been braided. It was tied instead in a loose ponytail. She wore blue tracksuit bottoms and a white sweater, but she still had her prayer beads wrapped around her wrist. The neighbours seemed to be returning to their homes and the room had quietened down. T.S. and his brother were gone as well; perhaps they were calling the police.

T.S.'s mother picked up a fish-man figure.

'You wanted to know about this creature?' she asked. 'When I was young, Grandpa used to tell me that it is the guide to a world where air is replaced by water and light is replaced by darkness. He called it the world of water. He said that it's a world where there are no barriers. He was quite obsessed and told everybody about it, especially the few travellers who stopped in our village on their way to Lhasa. He told them about how he was trying to go to the world of water. Do you two want some buttermilk tea?'

Jia Jia shook her head.

A world with no barriers, Jia Jia repeated to herself.

'I never got used to the taste of buttermilk tea. Even with a Tibetan wife,' said Ren Qi.

T.S.'s mother continued, her fingers running along her rice-coloured prayer beads.

'This couple in the photograph were good people. Kind. Grandpa spent a lot of time with them. The woman taught him how to make these little sculptures. But after they left, Grandpa stopped speaking altogether. I don't know what happened, but he stopped going on about the world of water. He kept making these little sculptures, you see. He even numbered them. The big one that you saw near the river, Grandpa made that too. It was the first one. But I know that even though he won't mention it, he's been trying to cross into that world all these years. I can tell, because he's continued to plant those tulips of his.'

'Tulips?' Ren Qi asked.

'We saw him planting them before we went to bed,' Jia Jia said.

'The tulips have never bloomed, that's why you haven't seen any,' T.S.'s mother explained. 'The old man is stubborn; he plants them every season. Even in the winter. According to Grandpa, the fish-like guide takes tulips in exchange for leading you to the world of water. Ever since Grandpa appeared in our village, he's been planting tulips every season. Perhaps he's gone to that world now. But I've checked, the flowers haven't grown.'

Silence reigned in the room. For a moment, the only sounds that could be heard were dogs barking outside, some near, some distant.

'You think that old people have been as they are for ever,' T.S.'s mother said. 'Doing those things they do, carving these figures and planting tulips. In reality, it's only been so many years. But you think they've been like that since the beginning of time.'

The woman inhaled deeply, and lingered a moment before letting the air out. Hunched over with strands of hair tucked behind her ears, she gazed into the distance, like an office worker on her subway ride home. Then she gave a smile that disappeared as suddenly as it came to her, and stood up from the bed. Ren Qi and Jia Jia followed suit.

'This all sounds like nonsense,' T.S.'s mother admitted, as the three of them walked in the direction of the door. 'But I'm glad I told you.'

'Can I keep the photo?' Jia Jia asked.

'I'm sure Grandpa wouldn't mind,' the woman said before descending the stairs.

15

Back in her room, tenderly unfolding the photo in her hand, Jia Jia kneeled on the wooden floor and faced the window. The mountains were sleeping beasts piled on top of each other; by this hour, the valley was beginning to form the shadow of a feeding bowl for those beasts. But it seemed as though the day would never stir.

'Wu Jia Jia,' Ren Qi said. 'Why do you think you've ended up here?'

Jia Jia rubbed her icy feet with her hands.

'I was there, in the world of water,' she said.

Ren Qi joined her on the floor with a loud thump.

'So it exists?' he asked.

'I've been there, I think,' Jia Jia told him. 'I don't know how.'

Ren Qi crossed his legs. 'Why are you still looking for the fish-man? If you've been to the world of water, you've seen him?'

'I haven't seen him there. I've only been inside the water. But every time, I've been afraid that I'd get stuck. It's as if the water knows. It'd spit me out.'

Ren Qi contemplated for a moment. A few times, he opened his mouth, wanting to say something, but decided against it and finally reached into his chest pocket for a cigarette.

After a few impatient puffs, he said, 'You know, when that woman was speaking, I couldn't help but think that my wife must be there in that world.'

Jia Jia took the cigarette from his fingers and smoked it.

'Why would she be there?' she asked.

'She's been gone for more than a month now.'

He wiped his forehead with his hand. Then he took the photo from Jia Jia and studied it.

'It's definitely a lousy photo.' He brushed it as if it were dusty, and handed it back.

'You don't know why your wife is missing, so you think she's in the world of water. It's because you don't understand it. We explain things that we don't understand by using other things we don't understand.'

'Wu Jia Jia, I don't think anything is chance. You believe in fate?'

Jia Jia did not respond.

'I do,' Ren Qi continued. 'I think it really must be fate that brought us here together, Wu Jia Jia. There must be a reason for me finding out about the world of water. I'm going to stay in this village, find the fish-man, plant tulips if I must, locate the world of water, and find my wife.'

He beamed like a child who believes he has found his way home. His teeth were stained yellow and his eyes were black lacquer. Jia Jia could see his suffering. It was the kind of torment still unfamiliar to the person in pain, the kind that induced more hope than resignation, the kind that would scar more deeply. He was still so young.

'All the uncertainty around your wife must be hard,' Jia Jia said.

'Pain is pain,' Ren Qi said calmly. 'There are various things that bring about pain, but in the end, we all feel it in the same way. These memories stick to you like the smell of tobacco on your fingers that won't wash away with soap.'

Silent for a few more seconds, Ren Qi said, 'Tell me more about the world of water.'

Jia Jia gave it some thought. It felt as though he was enquiring into something deeply private, as if he was asking her to take off her clothes and spread open her legs. For her to tell him what he wanted to hear, if she was even able to translate the experience into words, she would have to crack herself open like an egg and let the liquids spill out, leaving nothing for herself. But she could not refuse this man, she could not shut herself away this time. The moment she had found her hand wrapped in his as she swam in the cold, black water, her shell had already cracked. She gathered her words and began to speak.

'All I can tell you is this,' she said warily. 'In the world of water, if that's indeed where I've been, like I said there's nobody there. In that world, you disintegrate. Your body, your emotions, your perceptions and your thoughts are all separated into different components, like pages of a book that's been ripped apart. There is a fish there, a silver fish, but that's it. Everything else is just pitch-black. There is no other human. You're no longer human. So I can tell you that your wife is not there. Even if she is, you won't see her. Not in the way you're used to seeing her. She won't be looking for you either. It's a dreadfully empty place that is also overwhelmingly full. Do you understand what I'm getting at?'

Jia Jia looked up searchingly at Ren Qi.

'Sounds frightening,' Ren Qi commented.

'At first, it's frightening. Then you forget fear, and instead, you feel cold. Like ice that will never melt. I'm not talking about the bodily cold, but the sense that you will remain the same for ever, that nothing will change again. Do you know how that feels?'

Ren Qi pulled repeatedly on his earlobe.

'I thought my wife would always be with me,' he said. 'Like a character I've fallen in love with from my novel. I thought we'd always be the same us, in the same little apartment, eating the same porridge for breakfast, battling the same shower water that was either too hot or too cold. But now she's vanished, like pollen in the air. And nothing is the same any more. So to answer your question, no, I don't believe I know how it feels.'

Jia Jia nodded lightly. The sky was growing paler, though the sun was still nowhere to be seen.

'But to hell with all that. My plan is to find her. What's your plan, Wu Jia Jia?' Ren Qi asked.

'I'm going to leave,' Jia Jia said, surprised at how quickly she came to that decision. 'I don't think I will find any more answers here.'

Jia Jia gazed out at the gradually awakening world, pausing briefly at her awareness that nothing had stopped for Grandpa's disappearance. Wolves were going on their hunts, ants were building their nests, birds were fetching food for their hatchlings. And T.S.'s mother was already standing on the roof above the donkey shed, tossing hay at the animal.

Jia Jia traced her story in her head. Chen Hang's death had brought her here. She had met Grandpa, who knew about the world of water and made fish-man sculptures, but Grandpa had disappeared during the night. T.S.'s mother had given her this photo, and the couple in it must have had something to do with

Grandpa and the world of water. The fish-man takes tulips, but no tulips have blossomed.

She needed some sleep. Ren Qi seemed to sense this and, like an animal that had accidentally stepped into another's territory, he retreated to his side of the room and took out his notebook. He did not write anything, only opened it to a blank page and began stroking his chin. Jia Jia curled under the covers and turned away.

She imagined tulips. An entire field of them. She imagined that it was night, and the moon was radiating a pale, creamy light. The thousands of buds bloomed into white flowers, and one by one, the gradual opening up of each flower lulled Jia Jia a little deeper into sleep.

When Jia Jia packed up her things the following afternoon, Grandpa was still missing. Daylight had not brought him back. There seemed to have been an unspoken consensus in the village that if Grandpa had not returned by the next day, then his departure would somehow become permanent.

And now it was Jia Jia's turn to leave. T.S.'s family stood in front of their home and, waving their hands, told Jia Jia to visit again. She waved back and responded that she would. Disappearance, she thought, was really nothing more than departure without saying goodbye.

Ren Qi insisted on walking her to the car. Panting, he limped across the fields and up the hill.

'Where will you stay?' Jia Jia asked.

'I asked T.S. whether I could pay and stay in his house. But he knows my wife, so he brought me to her family. They told me that I can stay there for now,' Ren Qi said. 'I hadn't even met her parents before, until this morning.'

'Do they know where your wife is?'

'Her family had no idea. She hasn't contacted them, they told me. But don't you worry, I'll find the fish-man and my wife. Then I'll message you.'

'Sure.'

'Are you not going to pass by the river again?' Ren Qi asked.

Jia Jia shook her head. It was not about the log any more, that was only one of the many things that had directed her here. She would come back one day, she decided, to paint all of this. Perhaps she would ride an army-green motorbike as well, with her canvases strapped to the back. For a moment, she felt the mountains growing taller around her.

T.S. met her at the entrance of the village with his car boot already open. Before Jia Jia got in the car, Ren Qi gave her a pat on the shoulder. It was a warm, loving touch that rested there for a second longer than she had expected, as if something was flowing from him into her through his fingertips.

'Have a good flight back,' he said.

'Until next time,' Jia Jia said. The words came out of her with a certain stickiness, like honey being pulled out of a jar. She jerked open the car door.

Ren Qi adjusted the crutch under his armpit and said, 'Do you think your husband is there too? In the world of water? After all, he was the one who showed you the fish-man in the first place.'

Jia Jia paused. A group of children ran past on their way home from school. The image of Chen Hang kneeling in the bath with his forehead stuck to the bottom plunged itself into Jia Jia's mind. She shook her head decisively.

'He's dead,' she said, and climbed into the Jeep.

'That's right,' Ren Qi said in a tone that people used when they did not understand something but were fearful to ask again. He closed the door for her and took a step back from the car. A reserved smile hovered under his nose.

T.S. started the engine and manoeuvred a bit on the narrow road to turn the car around. Before they drove out, Jia Jia managed to catch a glimpse of the field where Grandpa had planted tulips less than twenty-four hours ago. T.S.'s mother was right, not a single leaf had grown there, even though Grandpa had been planting for years. As they turned the corner, the farmhouses disappeared one by one until Jia Jia could not see the village any more. And so began

an eight-hour drive through winding mountain roads;
a meditative drive. A left turn followed by a right
turn, repeatedly, until they lost track of how many
turns they had already made and how many they had
coming up. After a while, it felt as though they were
always driving on the same strip, and what was moving was the road below, not the car.

Jia Jia was on her way home, and her mind began
wandering back to Beijing, to Leo. She took out her
phone, but he had not messaged her since their last
meeting. She could picture him at the bar, hair gelled
back, wearing his bow tie, squeezing lemons. When
was the last time an image had brought her so much
comfort? It made her miss him terribly.

How long had she actually been gone? Counting the
time she had needed to finish up Ms Wan's painting
and arrange her travel documents, she realised she
had not seen Leo for more than a month. She had told
him that she did not want him to wait for her, and it
had been the right thing to say. But now, she wanted
to tell him about everything: the log, the stories she
had heard, the tulip bulbs, the writer she had met, the
photo.

The road was still weaving a net around the mountains. What if T.S. fell asleep? The car would tumble
down the cliff and both of them would die. There was
a good chance that nobody would find them in these
lost mountains; their bodies would merge with the

soil. If Leo was in fact waiting for her to return, she would disappoint him.

A sudden urgency for Beijing scratched at her heart. She had to be in the same city as Leo again, to know that if she walked in a certain direction, he would be there. These thoughts were like warm stones piling up inside her, and she closed her eyes and tried to still her mind.

16

Jia Jia pressed on the doorbell of her father's apartment. She took a deep breath.

When her plane landed, she had thought about going to Leo's bar, but instead had taken a taxi to her father's straight from the airport. She had not been there for more than two years. She wanted to speak with him, calmly, about his marriage, and tell him that she would give him back his money. She did not want to owe him. Since her father was now married to Xiao Fang, she imagined that his apartment would be carefully decorated with vases of flowers, colourful blankets, framed photographs and who knew, perhaps even a plump, spotted cat.

The door was the colour of black tea. It opened slowly, revealing her father in his blue pyjamas, holding a copy of *People's Daily* in his hand.

'Jia Jia!' At the sight of his daughter, he flung open the door. 'I didn't know you were back,' he said cheerfully, lifting his grey brows. Even Jia Jia was taken aback at how genuinely pleased he seemed. She forced a smile and pulled her suitcase inside.

'I thought I'd call in,' she said. 'Thanks for the money. Xiao Fang told me that it was from you. I haven't used it. I'd like to transfer it back.'

'Keep it. I know you need it,' said her father.

He bent over and fumbled through the shoe cabinet for a pair of slippers.

'I can just wear my socks,' Jia Jia said and sat on a chair to untie her shoelaces. 'I've found a tenant for the apartment. I'm OK for now.'

'You'll catch a cold. Xiao Fang taught me to always be careful not to let my feet get cold. Here you go.'

He placed a pair of red slippers in front of Jia Jia. As he turned and walked to the living room, she observed his back. If she had had a checklist for the symptoms of ageing, he would have had marks in every box. He was thinner, despite having grown a small, sagging belly. Though he had always been a man who kept his back straight, he was now hunching over a little, and as a result, his neck extended forward. The skin on his hands was folded and sprinkled with dark spots.

Xiao Fang was not at home, but her presence was everywhere. On the sandalwood bookshelves behind the sofa, there were several volumes on traditional medicine. Jia Jia's father only read history and philosophy. The remote controls for the television, DVD

player and music player were arranged neatly in a row
on top of the tea table, like soldiers sleeping in a camp.
In the corner of the room, there was a green yoga mat,
rolled up tidily and leaning against the wall. The room
smelt like essential oils. Lemon perhaps, or lime.

Funny, Jia Jia thought, that a woman could take
over a man's living space so effortlessly.

'Do you want to go out for dinner?' her father asked,
but he immediately seemed to change his mind and
said, 'Actually, why don't we stay at home? Xiao Fang
is away for the weekend. I'll cook something.'

'I can cook,' Jia Jia offered. She did not know that
her father could cook. She could not remember ever
eating anything that he had made.

'I haven't moved all day,' he said, pushing her shoulder to sit her down on the sofa. He handed her one of
the remote controls; the one in the middle. 'Watch
some TV or have a snooze. There's tea under the table.'

She looked at the clock. It was ten past five in the
afternoon.

'I'll go and buy some groceries,' he decided hur-
riedly and went into the bedroom to change. 'If you
want, you can start making the rice,' he shouted from
inside.

He soon emerged in a plain T-shirt and black trousers. After he took his car keys and closed the door
behind him, Jia Jia found the bag of rice in the kitchen
cupboard, measured out enough for the two of them,

washed it three times, and started the cooker. The phone rang in the living room and she rushed over reflexively. She watched it ring, unable to decide whether she should pick up. What if it was Xiao Fang? She did not want to speak to her. She told herself that if the person was still calling after five more rings, she would consider it an emergency and answer.

The phone went silent after three rings. Jia Jia watched it for a few more seconds, in case the person was going to call again, but there was only silence. Relieved, she sat on the sofa and took out the photo she had brought back from Tibet. Even from the back, she could tell that the man was young. And the woman, she seemed as light as a leaf. Jia Jia could hardly imagine that another living being was growing inside her.

Jia Jia decided that she would take a shower. It was delightful, she discovered, as she stepped under the hot water in the guest bathroom, to be able to clean herself thoroughly. She had not had a proper shower in days. Ever since she had arrived in T.S.'s village, cleaning herself had meant wiping her body with a towel. She shampooed her hair twice, lathered her skin repeatedly with soap, and stood under the showerhead for a long time.

When she had finished, she found that her father had returned and was busy chopping carrots. Jia Jia leaned against the sofa and let the air conditioner blow gently on her for a while. She started to feel cold, and turned to the bookshelves for something to busy herself with. Nietzsche, Rousseau, Diderot, Sun Tzu and others lined the shelves along with dozens of books on the Liao dynasty, an era that had particularly interested her father ever since he was a child. He could never explain why he had such a fondness for this dynasty; everyone else found it rather bizarre. The Tang dynasty, the Warring States, or the Qing dynasty – these had many more gripping stories.

Jia Jia was not interested in anything she could see. She was not about to pick up *The Social Contract* and begin reading. She migrated towards the other end of the shelf and spotted, in front of another collection of burgundy history books, a palm-sized stone figure. It was the fish-man, standing among the other little ornaments on the shelf like a curious souvenir. She froze for a moment. Why would her father have this? Why had she not seen it before? *Had* she in fact seen it before? Jia Jia fell into a moment of stunned wordlessness and her body suddenly felt weak. She tried to steady herself. She turned the fish-man around to find the back bare, without a number. This figure, unlike the ones she had seen in the village, was expertly crafted.

'Wash your hands! Almost finished here!' her father yelled over the sounds of fresh vegetables being tossed into heated oil.

Startled by his voice, Jia Jia instinctively stuffed the fish-man into her pocket. Her father appeared from the kitchen with a dish in each hand.

'Get the rice,' he said. 'And chopsticks.'

She did as she was told.

Jia Jia sat at the table and studied her father, thinking about the figure in her pocket. Her father's hands, holding the chopsticks, were slightly unsteady – something that she had first noticed years ago when he took her out to lunch, but tonight, it made her heart clench and tremble.

On the table sat a plate of braised pork belly, a little dark in colour, with slightly too much oil floating on top. The other dish was stir-fried carrots and fungus, perfectly bright in colour, cooked more skilfully.

Her father, using his chopsticks like a spoon, scooped up a piece of pork and carefully hovered it over Jia Jia's bowl, and then finally allowed it to drop inside. 'Try this.'

Jia Jia held the bowl in her hand and gazed down at the lonely piece of pork.

'Try it,' repeated her father. 'You like braised pork, don't you?'

She picked it up and stuffed it into her mouth. Although she expected it to be rather salty from having been bathed in too much soy sauce, it actually tasted too sweet.

Her father smiled in a satisfied way and pointed his chopsticks at the window. 'If I had gone five minutes later, the supermarket would've run out of pork belly. I remember you used to ask for braised pork every day when you were a girl. Pork belly tastes best when braised. Eat some more. I'm sure you got sick of the food in Tibet and started missing home-cooked food after a few days.'

The last time Jia Jia had sat at home and eaten dinner with her father was the day before he left. What did they eat? She tried to investigate the deep cave of her memory but could not recall a single dish on the table that day. She stuffed another piece of pork into her mouth, chewed a few times, and before she could swallow it she had put in another.

Then, utterly unprepared, she found herself crying hysterically. She was like a fallen child who had kept her tears contained until her parents took her into their embrace, releasing a sundering, burning wail. She nodded several times while she sobbed, signalling to her father that he was right – she did like braised pork belly. She hoped that he understood her nods, as she could no longer put any words together. Jia Jia had lost all control. There was not a single string that she could pull to stop herself from this crying that seemed as though it was never going to end.

Her father did not move. Still holding the bowl of rice in his big hands, he listened to her.

Time either froze or passed quickly; Jia Jia thought that it could have been either. As the tears gushed out of her, she felt herself shrinking down like a bar of soap, losing her original form. She had become a shapeless and authentic version of herself. This change, she knew, was going to be irrevocable.

And then, all of a sudden, like a speeding car that had crashed into a large tree, it stopped. For a while, neither of them spoke. In that apartment, there was no tension any more, no surging of emotions; neither was there any sense of solace. What was there, under a warm light, was a meal shared between father and daughter.

When they had both finished their rice, Jia Jia looked her father straight in the eye.

'Ba,' she said with unwavering determination. 'Tell me about the fish-man.'

He gazed back at her with an alarmed expression, which then morphed into a worried one that finally became composed, gentle and firm. He put down his chopsticks, reached for a box of tissues, handed this to Jia Jia, and crossed his arms on the table.

'What would you like to know?' he asked.

The last vestiges of nervousness had vanished from Jia Jia. Control came back to her and her mind was clear as glass. She was going to find out why her father had a fish-man figure; to proceed was as natural to her now as it was for coconuts to fall when fully ripe. She fetched the figure from her pocket and placed it in front of her father, along with the photo taken by Grandpa.

'I found this on the shelf,' Jia Jia said steadily. 'I've seen fish-man sculptures like this at a village I visited in Tibet.' She pointed to the photo. 'This village.'

Her father sank back into his seat with his arms still crossed in front of his chest. For a time, nothing came out from his mouth and he just stared at the photo. Then he straightened his back, leaned forward and chose his words carefully.

17

'If I had it my way, I'd never speak about it. These memories have been like a hole in the ground, right beneath the steps to my door. On rainy days there would be a puddle, and I'd always step around it. Sometimes, there'd be relentless storms, and I'd stay inside and watch the hole fill up and overflow. Long periods of time would also come when the hole would be dry and almost unnoticeable. And then, without warning, it would rain again. But throughout the years, I have come to accept that the world spins, one season pours into another, and the past travels full circle back to you. So I'll tell you everything I know, Jia Jia, because I owe it to you, and to your mother. But also, more importantly, I'll tell you because maybe then you will understand.

'First of all, let me prelude this story by saying that I have never seen the fish-man or the world of water. As such, I do not know what it is. And to this day, I cannot say whether I'm grateful for that. But all this is not to tell you that it has no effect on me. No, no. On the contrary, my life has been governed by the world of water since the day I came to know about it, or maybe even before I became aware that it had flooded into your mother, thirty years ago.

'At the time when I met your mother, she was struggling to become a sculptor and I was a very average man. Why, of all art forms, she chose sculpting, I do not know. How and where she learned to sculpt, she never told me either. But she had her mind set on becoming a sculptor, and no one was ever going to convince her to change. I got to know her the first week after Chinese New Year, at the Ditan temple fair. Her head popped up from the sea of people directly into my vision: she was standing on a bench, searching for a sugar sculpture stand, which I eventually helped her find. She wore a large, brown ushanka-hat that covered half of her face. It belonged to her father, she told me later, who had received it as a gift from a teacher during his studies in the Soviet Union. Your mother wore it every day in the winter, and during most of the dates we went on, I was barely able to see her properly. As a result, for a long time I had no idea what her hair looked like. But that only added to her charm and made her even more desirable.

'I had never met anyone like her before. She daydreamed, her thoughts would often run wildly. One minute, she might be speaking about different kinds of beer, and the next, she would be reciting poetry. She was a woman who would jump into frozen lakes naked or ride her bike into the suburbs in the middle of the night. She was the opposite of me and none of our friends could imagine us being lovers. But after a few months, we got married, and she became my entire world.

'All I wanted thereafter was to live a lifetime with her, where every day I'd return to a home that smelt like fresh noodles, and she would greet me with a face that always bloomed like a daisy when I opened the door. As long as I had her, I didn't care about the hardships of life. She was like a pair of shoes that fitted perfectly, wrapping me up, keeping me warm. We lived in a sixty-square-metre two-bedroom apartment that was comfortably big enough for the two of us. It faced the south and kept us warm in the winter and cool in the summer. More than enough light shone into our living space during the day, and seeing the way your mother hummed different tunes and held a bottle of beer in her hand while she worked on her sculptures, I deemed that she was content.

'But as time passed, I came to gradually forget who she was and what she wanted. Or hell, I admit I most likely didn't even know in the first place. She dreamed of something much bigger than our apartment and our placid lives within it. She wanted to be outside. Still, she stayed with me and pretended that the life I had designed for us was the one she wanted as well. Of course, I was unaware of any of this at the time and my vision only gradually cleared later, after we decided to have a baby.

'A few months into our marriage, we tried for a child. I can't remember whose idea it was in the first place, but one of us must have decided that he or she wanted a child, and the other person must have agreed. It was the natural thing to do anyway. We worked on this mission for months but nothing happened. At first, we didn't think too much about it all and agreed that luck was not on our side. We carried on with our lives. I went to work as usual while your mother stayed at home and made all sorts of sculptures. But ever so slowly, our failure to make a child began to infiltrate our lives like water seeping through walls. Your mother began to sob whenever she got her period. Although nothing had changed, the apartment started to feel empty, as if we once had a child and now the child was gone. A thick, dark cloud was taking shape and expanding, gnawing at us in our sleep. At some point, I noticed that your mother was making sculptures of children she saw out on the streets. She told me that she didn't even remember when and why she had started doing that.

'It was as if we had been cursed, and soon enough, the curse began to manifest itself physically. Things started to break – the kitchen light, the heater, the radio, your mother's gold earrings, my most expensive pair of shoes. One morning, on your mother's way to the vegetable market, the sun was shining brighter than usual, so she decided to remove her ushanka-hat to immerse herself in the warm winter day. A few seconds later, a stray dog snatched the hat from her hands and ripped it in half, right there, before running off never to be seen again. She came home and wept, forgetting entirely about the market. I had tinned food for dinner that night, and your mother didn't eat at all. Each day she slept less and less, which put me on edge and gave me sweats and nightmares. She'd wake up at dawn and stare out the window for hours, like a floating spirit that had lost all those who had known her in her lifetime. At first, I'd get up too to comfort her, but eventually I just pretended to be asleep.

'It all became even worse when two of our friends gave birth at around the same time. One girl, one boy. Your mother locked herself inside the apartment for a week: she wouldn't speak to anyone, not even to her own mother and sister. Finally, a close friend of mine at work gave me an idea. He found a doctor who agreed to tell your mother that negative moods had dire consequences on fertility and that she mustn't allow herself to be so gloomy. That worked. The next day, as though nothing had happened, your mother began eating and sleeping normally again. She offered to take care of our friends' babies, for which our friends were delightedly grateful and called her a kind-hearted woman. She soon became known around the neighbourhood as the childless woman who ran a nursery in her home. As a result, during the day, our apartment was always bursting with the frantic wailing or laughing sounds of children who weren't our own. But once nightfall came, an unendurable silence fell upon our home.

'This continued for a while. Even though the crisis seemed to be over, we both knew that there was a wound below the surface that was festering and corroding our minds, and if things continued the way they were, one day, both of us would be nothing but empty, fractured shells.

'I suppose the other thing that became different in our day-to-day lives was that your mother began to read. A lot. She immersed herself in all sorts of books. When she started reading a book, she wouldn't stop until she finished the entire thing. She read Chinese novels, European classics, poems, books of quotations from famous people, newspapers – pretty much anything legible she could lay her hands on.

'One winter afternoon, out of the blue, while I was tossing some cabbage into a pan and she was reading *Jane Eyre*, she looked up at me and announced that she was going to Tibet and wanted me to go with her. It was impossible, I laughed. It was too far, and we didn't have the time or money. How ludicrous. But she was entirely serious. I could tell from the way she widened her eyes and held her hands in fists. I never found out whether her decision had anything to do with *Jane Eyre*, though I can't imagine how those two things could have been related.

'Though it was not easy, I still managed to take a month off. She sold her bicycle and we used our savings to buy an army motorbike to be picked up in Chengdu. We barely packed anything, only some thick clothes, a duvet, a tent we borrowed, and some basic cooking equipment.

'A few days before we were supposed to leave, we found out that your mother was pregnant. I felt as though everything was going to be wonderful again. Your mother, with you growing inside her, was the most prized treasure to me, and I became excessively protective. I asked an acquaintance to bring all kinds of natural supplements from Hong Kong, fearing that your mother was not getting enough nutrients. When I came home with the bags of supplements, she began to cry, saying that we needed to save money for the trip.

'I wasn't going to let her go to Tibet. She was far too delicate for such a journey. What if we lost our hard-earned child? Whose responsibility would it be? Did she understand how difficult it would be for us to find an adequate hospital if we were in the wild? But your mother said she knew, she knew better than anybody, and she wanted to protect her child more than I could ever imagine. But she needed the trip just as much as she needed our child, she told me. She was set in her own ways and refused to budge an inch. She spewed out a series of accusations, calling me self-centred, overbearing, ignorant and limited. She told me that I was a man without dreams and didn't even understand hers. What was her dream? We were finally going to have a child. Wasn't that what she wanted?

'When she saw that I was perplexed, the exact words that came out of her mouth were these: "I must have this child, but I must also go on this trip. Otherwise, I'll be eternally caged in this apartment, for this life and my following lives, like you, caught in the delusion that there is some sort of meaning to all this. But we live in a far larger reality."

'For the first and only time, I slapped her, across the face.

'Neither of us had the heart to cook dinner that day. We refused to speak to each other. Your mother continued to prepare for the trip, though I wasn't sure who she had in mind as a substitute driver if I insisted on staying. It turned out that the day came, and nobody showed up. She grabbed everything, including my clothes, and headed for the train station. She didn't have a motorbike licence, but once she arrived in Chengdu, she would have ridden off regardless, with or without me. I knew her well enough. Her determination frightened me, and out of what was most likely my male instinct to protect my wife and my unborn child, I yielded and took over the luggage.

'During our trip, we did come close to death, more than once, due to landslides or rain. Once, we encountered a wolf pack in the mountains while we were camping at night. We were terrified: we secured ourselves inside our tent and prayed for safety. Another time, our bike tumbled over while we were taking a curve, and your mother was thrown off, injuring her shoulder. There weren't any health stations nearby but we were close to a small town. We knocked on every door, and luckily we found a man, an ex-combat medic, who was willing to help us.

'For many nights, I watched your mother's back as she stood ruminating in the darkness of the wild mountains, taking short breaths under a star-filled sky that seemed as though we'd be able to touch it if only we jumped. Her thoughts were silent, and I never mustered the courage to ask her about them. We didn't fight again, nor did we talk much.

'We never made it to Lhasa. We stopped for two weeks at a small village. It already seemed to me like we were at the edge of the world. Your mother was having severe reactions to the harsh conditions on the road, yet she continued to insist on travelling deeper into Tibet. She would hug me and say that only when she had gone as far as she could would she be able to return home with me. I didn't question this, because I had come to see that I should never have tried to apply my understanding of things to her. She was a different human being, after all. I made up my mind to accompany her on this journey, to the very end, and then bring her back home with me. I told myself that I was being selfless, and what I was doing was for love. So I believed her unconditionally, or at least kept that facade, when she came racing back to the farmhouse, on the second night we spent at the village, and told me about the world she had plunged into.

'She said, with her eyes wide, that she had met a creature, a man with the body of a fish, near the river. It wasn't big but it wasn't small either. It measured about a metre long, she told me, and it was swimming in the air, just high enough for her not to be able to reach it. Behind the creature, there was darkness. At first, the darkness resembled black curtains drawn across an unlit stage, and the creature was whirling in front of it, under the spotlight. After a moment, once her eyes adjusted, she could faintly discern the movement of water. The creature turned away from her and swam into the water behind, and your mother, fearless as she was, followed.

'Inside, it was black and infinite, she recalled, as though she was at once trapped in the core of the earth but also floating freely in outer space. Though this was an inaccurate description, she added, because the real sensation of being in those waters was incomparable to anything else she could imagine. I prodded for more, and finally, after many stuttering attempts at giving me an answer, she arrived at the conclusion that her reality had become nothing but water. This baffled me even more.

'How did she get out? I wanted to know.

'"I just swam," she told me.

'Where did the creature go? Were there other creatures? If it was a sea, I reasoned, there must have been other organisms.

'"The creature disappeared as soon as I entered," she responded. "And then there was nothing at all, not a single fish. Not even light. It was the most frightening yet beautiful experience."

'The following day, she gathered the villagers and told them what had happened. She wanted to see if others had seen it too. Most of her audience were just as perplexed as I was. The children listened intently as if being told a fairy tale, but left to play as soon as she finished. But one man became particularly fascinated. He was a bald man with a piercing look, about sixty or so, who claimed that he had been searching for what he called "the world of water" for as long as he

could remember. The villagers addressed him as
Grandpa. All day long, Grandpa followed your mother
and asked her questions. What did the creature look
like? What did she mean, man's head and fish's body?
So your mother began making these sculptures for
him, carving them out of anything she could find
around the village.

'"Here," she would tell him. "This looks about right."

'Your mother and Grandpa marched down to the
river every night in search of the world of water, but
not a single time did they come across it or the creature again. Disappointed, they'd return to the farmhouse early in the morning, sit around the table, and
carve more of these sculptures while discussing this
new world that had been forced into our lives.

'Once, while they were carving, I asked Grandpa
how he had come to know about this world. He told
us that in the mountains where he was from, there
used to be an abundance of wild tulips. Unlike the
ones we knew, these tulips had larger petals. They'd all
bloom overnight and occupy entire fields, and then
they would all wither together again, as if they were
nothing but a fleeting dream. Rarely would you spot
two different-coloured tulips in the same field. The
beauty of it all was difficult to put into words, he said
wistfully.

'The first time Grandpa heard about the world of
water, he was still a child. Someone had tripped on

a rock amidst a field of white tulips and tumbled into that world. The man came back shivering, frightened like a beaten dog. After that day, the man who fell into the world of water would never again leave the farmhouse alone. If he had to go somewhere, he would take a yak with him. Whenever that man was forced to remember the world of water, all he said was, *It's black, it's black.* However, none of this frightened young Grandpa. He felt that an invisible string had been woven during the years of his past life and the lives before that, and that the purpose of his current life was to continue extending the string. He made up his mind to look for the world of water. To him, it was not even a choice, but a destiny of some sort.

'As the years passed, the man who had seen the world of water died, and people gradually forgot about the entire thing. Grandpa, however, went to the tulip fields every day. Until one particular sorrowful year, when the tulips didn't grow. Not a single one. The year that happened, Grandpa had just turned thirteen and lost all his family members in a kitchen fire. It was as if the tulips had taken with them everything from his life, and he came to understand what it meant to be truly alone, and the fact that life was ever-changing. He sat in the mountains for three days and three nights, staring at the bare fields, hearing the wolves howl up at the moon.

'Then he left, in search of the one last thing that he still had – the world of water.

'"Why did you stop here?" we asked him.

'"It felt like home," Grandpa answered.

'Afterwards, your mother and I began gathering tulips for a few days. We took our motorbike and spent all our mornings out in the mountains, searching for those wild flowers. To our surprise, these tulips were not rare, and we were able to find quite a large quantity of them. Just as in Grandpa's memory, they grew densely, filling up entire fields. Your mother picked anything she came across – white, yellow, red, blue, purple, you name it. As long as it was a tulip, she brought it home with her. We filled the room up with these beautiful flowers.

'But things took an unexpected turn. I could never have imagined that one rainy afternoon, in that little Tibetan village, amid the honey-like scent of blooming tulips, I would lose my entire world.

'That day, your mother woke up from a nap and found herself submerged in the world of water. I was there in the room too, but there's a blank white spot in my memory. No matter how hard I try to think back to that afternoon, all I remember is the two of us going to bed for a nap, and the mist blanketing over the village. Then what I recall, clear as the sound of a trumpet, is the moment when I opened my eyes and saw the tears all over your mother's face, the blood oozing from the cuts on her arms, and the knife she held at her throat.

'"What on earth are you doing?" I asked her.

'"Kill me," she said.

'I told her to give me the knife. She made me promise to kill her. I begged her to calm down, and asked her why she wanted to die. I assured her that we were going to go home. It would all be over soon.

'"It's already over," she said calmly, tears still rolling down her face. "My body is still here, but it won't be for long. The thing that gives this body meaning has been taken by the water. It's hollowing me out. I left a part of myself there. It's going to take all of me eventually."

'I didn't believe her. More accurately, I couldn't fathom the meaning behind her words. I called her selfish, for thinking only about herself and not our family. I knew that I was attempting to handcuff her with my idea of family again. I told myself that keeping her alive was enough to make a family.

'I regret it all. I regret not being able to hold her hand and pull her back from the world of water. I keep thinking that had I been more understanding, had I accepted her way of living, things would've turned out differently and she would've found something to hold on to. But I was foolish. I couldn't pull her back, even if I tried. Your mother said that there was nothing in the world of water, but I have come to the understanding that all she ever wanted was there, in those deep waters. And she left me alone here, in this world, searching for whatever it is I want.

'I grabbed the knife from her by force. Grandpa must have heard our quarrel and seen your mother with that knife. Because from that day on, until we left, he didn't speak another word about the world of water.

'We returned home, and after a few months, your mother gave birth to you. She loved you with an intensity that I had never seen in her love before. I can say for certain that you were the only reason she held on to this family for all those years. She took on the role of the mother I had always believed her to be. Whatever was left of her, she gave it all to you. But during this time, I watched her drift from me, getting lost further in a world that I've never come to know. I learned that there are two kinds of people: those who need boundaries, and those who will die from them. Making your mother live the way I wanted us to be together was no less cruel than keeping a fish in a bowl.

'It was an incredibly lonely experience for us both, I believe. Apart from living in the same space and sharing a child, we had nothing else in common. Throughout those years, she didn't speak about going back to Tibet. Occasionally, she'd mention the world of water, but never anything more than a brief remark.

Sometimes she'd buy tulips, and together we'd watch them flower and fade.

'Finally, we left each other. Not long after I moved out, I learned about her illness. In a way, those cancer cells were not very different from that knife she held in her hand, just manifested in a different way. They killed her.

'All my life, I've made countless mistakes. I've done plenty of things that I still question. But there is one thing I did that I would certainly do again, which was to take that knife from her hand.

'She was wrong, you see, the world of water couldn't take all of her. Things don't work in such absolute ways. But she never understood this. Parts of her, like seeds, have been planted on this earth and grown into shoots, flowers, trees, day by day. The roots have dug deep into the soil and will continue to extend, for as long as you and I can imagine. Do you really think that the body can be separated from the rest of us? I certainly don't.

'This has been a long story, I apologise. I'm not going to ask you whether you've seen the world of water. I think I know the answer already. And I'm not surprised that something brought you back to that village we knew. But for reasons I can't quite put my finger on, I don't sense from you any remnants of that total darkness that your mother fell into. For that, I am glad.

'Keep this little sculpture. Your mother made it. We should visit her some day. I don't think we've ever been to her grave together. We'll bring some beer. She quite enjoyed beer.'

18

The moon resembled a circular pendant on a chain of three stars. Nights in Beijing were still cool blessings, and Jia Jia untied her hair and allowed it to hang down her back, protecting her neck from the breeze. Early spring's lime leaves had turned to a palette of lush green, and gingko leaves waved in the wind like miniature hand fans.

Li Chang had been released shortly after the May holidays. Jia Jia's aunt decided that it did not matter if they were a few days late: they would celebrate the holiday together as a family. After dinner, at Li Chang's request, Jia Jia had gone to drop off a bag of zongzi at Mr Du's for the upcoming Duanwu festival. Mr Du was alone at home, watching television. He had not covered up the wall painting. In a few weeks, he had become an old man. Jia Jia could see the despair in his face, the loneliness of a silent apartment at night. She gave him the zongzi, and he thanked her politely for them and gave her a can of white tea in return. They did not exchange many more words, and afterwards, Jia Jia ambled to the Central Business District.

Knowing that Li Chang was returning home, Jia Jia had contacted her estate agent to find a small studio apartment on the east side of town. Her aunt, meanwhile, liberated and excited, had gone to the flower market and bought red fish and red coral for the aquarium. For the past few chaotic days at her grandmother's home, Jia Jia had been painting. She had begun working on another rendition of the horse on the beach, on a bigger canvas this time. It had kept her busy, and tonight was the first time that she had set foot outside. She had not seen Leo yet; she needed some time to piece the world of water together and absorb her father's story. It was enough for her to know that he was nearby.

She came across an empty playground and stepped into the sand, careful not to get any into her shoes. Rocking herself back and forth on a swing, Jia Jia glanced up at the building in front of her and counted the windows until she located her apartment. It was the day her tenants were due to move in. The apartment was brightly lit, and there was a young couple and an older woman sitting around a table right by the window. The walls seemed bare – they must not have had much time to set up their furniture. The young couple looked about the same age as Jia Jia. Even from their sitting positions, she could tell that the woman was taller than the man. The man had his back towards the window. He was engaged in conversation with the elderly woman, who must have been one of their mothers – his, most likely. He was leaning into his chair, lifting a beer bottle up to his mouth every few seconds.

All of a sudden, the three of them turned their heads towards the bedroom, appearing alarmed. The young woman stood up and scuttled across the living room towards the back, returning soon with a baby in her arms and a half-embarrassed, half-proud smile across her face.

Jia Jia's phone vibrated in her bag. It was a message from Ren Qi.

How have you been, Wu Jia Jia? I hope you're with your family, eating some Beijing food and drinking plenty of wine. I'm getting quite sick of Tibetan food. I'm still here, sitting on the dirt road near the river, with a bottle of qingke wine next to me. Oh, how quiet it is tonight! Do you want to hear something? T.S. told me that when he was a child, there used to be wild tulips growing in this area. Where do you think they all went? There's nothing here now. Just rocks and water.

Jia Jia imagined him sitting alone on a small road, his crutch and notebook lying next to him, under the same moon that was above her head. She pictured the moon in Tibet to be lower and more brilliant, as if with a slight push it would bounce like a ball from one mountain to another.

After a minute, another message followed:

I wanted to call you, but I couldn't let myself interrupt this silence. Plus, I'd rather not listen to my own voice right now. I hope you're getting far in your search for the world of water.

Jia Jia thought for a moment before she began typing:

When are you coming back? Have you found your wife yet? When you come back, let's meet, and I'll tell you everything.

After she had sent the message, she placed the phone on her lap. Then she bent down and took off her shoes, digging her toes into the cool sand. She thought about the world of water and how she had been there already, long ago, when her mother was pregnant with her. Perhaps, like her mother, she had left something there too. As her father had told her his story, she had understood that the couple in the photograph were him and her mother. How caring he looked; his hand holding her mother's arm as if afraid that she would get blown away with the wind. Jia Jia had no memories of seeing such intimacy between them. She could not have imagined that a single gesture like a hand on an elbow could give her so much comfort.

Jia Jia's phone vibrated again:

I'm not well. Devastated. My wife has returned, but with another man, a Tibetan stud she knew growing up. You should've seen her face when she saw me here, waiting like a fool, trying to bring her back from some world of water that I'd never seen before. You know what I did? I smiled at her. She didn't even want to talk to me.

Jia Jia read his last message over a few times. It pinched at something inside her, knowing that he had not been armed for this, thinking about how much it must have wounded him.

But this is life, isn't it? his next message said. *Sometimes you want to dance, sometimes you want to cry. I'm not crying though. The pain is too fresh. I can't cry. Not until I see her bookmarked novel on our shelf, or open the half-finished tin of her oolong tea, or find her lipstick under our bed. Until then, I'm not going to feel anything apart from shame. But when the time comes, my heart will tear. I know it. I'm going back to the village now. I have run out of alcohol.*

She took a deep breath and looked back up at her apartment and the family, beginning their new lives in the place she had left behind. The playground remained empty, the yellow slide dispirited, holding up for no one in the dark. Jia Jia began typing:

Have you been writing lately? I realised that I've never asked you for the titles of your books. It'd be nice, I think, if I could get my hands on a copy of one. Ren Qi, I've come to conclude that sometimes, the easiest way to lose somebody for ever is to keep them around.

Before she'd finished, her phone vibrated again:

The tulips! Wu Jia Jia, you wouldn't believe what I'm seeing. That empty field is now filled with pure white tulips! They're glowing like they belong in the palace up there, in the skies. The wind is gently combing their petals. The entire field is swaying like silk. Looking up at the full moon tonight, I can't help but imagine this is what the moon goddess's blanket must look like. Wu Jia Jia, allow me to announce to you, the tulips have flowered!

In front of Jia Jia, the world of water came ink black, devouring the street lamps, the moon, the yellow slide, the apartment building and the family inside. The pavement washed away. The sand beneath Jia Jia's feet spread sparsely into the water. Beijing was slipping its bounds.

The sudden cold struck her. No amount of clothing or fire could warm her up, she knew. She sank, or so she believed, and focused on her body's descent, refrained from struggling. This way, she hoped, perhaps she could at last find a bottom to this world. *Because that's what we do, isn't it?* she thought. *Hope.*

The fish-man wiggled into view. Its face, like in Chen Hang's sketch, showed nothing particularly intriguing. It was the face of an average man, with features that were medium-sized, wearing a blank expression. The most noteworthy part was perhaps the bald head that, at the neck, morphed into the khaki-coloured, scaled body. It was certainly not an exceptionally beautiful creature. It opened its mouth to speak.

'Come home, dinner is waiting on the table,' it said in a cello voice as it swam from side to side, as if between two invisible walls.

'Is my mother there?' Jia Jia asked. 'She was here, thirty years ago.'

'You'll have to find out for yourself. Now come on.' The fish-man was becoming agitated, its fins kept tapping on the side of its body.

'I can tell you this,' it added. 'If she's not where you are, she might be where I am.'

Jia Jia began moving her legs. They felt heavy, as though they had been frozen solid. The fish-man twirled around and zoomed into the darkness; Jia Jia tailed behind. Soon, she could not see the fish-man's head any more, only the tip of its tail, swaying.

She wanted to speak to the fish-man some more, but nothing came out. Was she moving her lips? It was difficult enough to keep up with its speed, let alone hold a conversation. She could not even decide what she was trying to say.

At some point, she realised that she must have closed her eyes, or fallen asleep for a moment while treading water. The fish-man was nowhere – when had it disappeared? Her memory was failing her, dissolving like salt into the water. The coldness had also vanished, her senses were failing, her body that was once heavy as stone was now light as foam. She ran her hands over herself.

Nothing. There was nothing. Her body was gone. In fact, what she had believed were her hands were no more than a thought. This must be the end of it all. Was she ever going to be able to have a cigarette again? She desperately wanted one. She checked for her bag. Surely, it was not there.

Was this how her mother got trapped? Was 'trapped' even the right word? Maybe this was how reincarnation worked. She would wake up in the body of another, and live a different life; in all likelihood, in her new life, she would never find out about the world of water. She might not even be human. She remembered the painting on Ms Wan's wall. Mr Du's wall now. The sapphire bowl glowing in the centre of it, held between the Buddha's hands. The dash of orange that she had added into the blue paint.

'What are you doing?' The fish-man's voice emerged from the darkness.

'I must have lost you,' Jia Jia said, pulled out of her trance.

'Keep up.'

'I can't see you,' Jia Jia said, wondering how it was possible for them to hear each other.

'Just follow my voice.'

Jia Jia did her best to trace the source of the voice. It seemed to come from above her.

'Maybe you can sing a song,' she said. 'So that I can follow.'

The fish-man began humming a tune. It was not anything recognisable or pleasant to listen to, but that was not its purpose anyway. Jia Jia instructed her bodiless self to close her eyes, to swim faster, not to lose the fish-man.

'This isn't going to work. I'm not moving,' Jia Jia said. 'I don't have a body.'

The fish-man stopped in the middle of its song and said, 'I don't either. That's why you can't see me. But I can assure you that we're still moving. We're always moving.'

'Can you tell me where we are going?' asked Jia Jia.

'When we stop moving, we will have arrived at our destination.'

Jia Jia listened to the fish-man's droning tune as her thoughts waned. What language was it singing in? Tibetan? It did not matter, because eventually, the sound of the singing faded too.

Nothingness.

Only the silence of the mind.

In the distance, she thought she saw a faint light. A silver fish.

19

Jia Jia saw her mother's dim, orange lantern glowing at the entrance of Leo's bar. It was not hung up, but instead sat on top of a small round table that Leo must have recently acquired. A beige cloth was set over the table and an empty ashtray was arranged next to the lamp. There was also a wooden chair, for smokers who preferred to sit down. Jia Jia touched her fingers along the contours of her face and watched her own reflection in the window of the bar. It was her, in the flesh, that was for certain. She turned around and located her apartment over the road. Her tenants were still at the table, the man drinking his beer, the woman smiling with the baby in her arms. The sound of an electric scooter grew louder and then weakened as it travelled into the distance.

At this time of the year, Beijing was particularly dry. The world of water had left no visible trace, but it stayed with Jia Jia as though running through her blood.

She lit a cigarette. The guard at the car park had been replaced by another young, shorter man. This one, like his predecessor, also had his head buried in his phone. He wore thick-rimmed glasses, the peak of his cap turned slightly towards one side. Jia Jia thought that she could see him smiling.

The door opened and Leo emerged from behind it. He had a scarf hung on his arm, which he wrapped around Jia Jia's shoulders.

'I saw you from the window,' he said, taking a cigarette from her pack.

'I came back a few days ago,' she responded.

'New tenants?' Leo pointed up at her apartment window.

Jia Jia smiled. 'They've just moved in. Looks like a lovely family. Are you closing the bar soon?'

'There are still plenty of customers inside.' He turned back to look at his bar. Tobacco and citrus from his tall, slim figure touched Jia Jia softly on the nose.

She put her cigarette out in the new ashtray and steadied her gaze on a tree in the distance. A bird had just flown back to its nest. She thought it must have ventured far, to return at this time. She drew the scarf tighter across her chest and waited, without a tinge of urgency to be anywhere or do anything, for Leo to finish his cigarette.

*

Later Jia Jia sat on the stool at the end of the counter and sipped brandy until the bar closed. The customers kept Leo busy all night. He smiled at them, took their orders, made their drinks, settled their bills. Groups of friends sat together, speaking in different accents, downing one drink after another around the low, circular tables, laughing sometimes, and then finally trickling out the door, some turning north, others south. Leo wiped the tables and waited for the next group of people to occupy them. This city was much like that, Jia Jia thought, with people coming and going, some staying briefly, others longer. And as one person left, the city waited for the next to take her place.

As the evening passed, it gradually became clear to Jia Jia what the world of water had left behind. There was something incredibly light inside her, like a cloud on a clear night, a dandelion seed in the air, a ballet dancer, Ravel's *Jeux d'eau*. If the world of water had taken something away from her, it must have been something heavy.

She thought about Ren Qi, about the village, the smell of goat's butter and incense, about what he was doing amid the field of white tulips, his face peachy from that bottle of qingke wine. She would respond to his text messages tomorrow, and tell him about the fish-man and the world of water.

Jia Jia lifted her glass a little, toasting those who were far away.

When she set the glass down, her thoughts wended their way back home. Tomorrow, she decided, she would be painting the sea.